WARDEN AND THE ASSASSIN

THE GRAE SISTERS

BOOK ONE

EVE LANGLAIS

Prologue

·)·)·)·⊙·(·(·(·

MY EYES POPPED open before my alarm, my excitement bubbling. Turning sixteen only happened once in a girl's life. Add in the fact that not only did it land on a Friday the 13th but also on the day of a rare hybrid eclipse, making it extra special —for me and my sisters.

Triplets born, one after another, at the exact moment the moon covered the sun. Was it any wonder our mother, Fraussa Grae—which she swore was her real name—already a little bit too much into the esoteric, chose to name us after the weird Graeae sisters of Greek mythology? You

1

know the gross ones that shared an eyeball. Enyo, Deino, and Pemphredo. Of us, only I, Enyo, kept my original name. My sisters went by the nick-names, Dina and Frieda. In their defense, no one ever spelled their birth names right.

That special morning, we dressed, each of us catering to our unique sense of style. For me that consisted of jeans and a rock band T-shirt with un-laced black boots. My usual attire that caused my more fashion-conscious sister to sigh. "Could you at least do something about your hair?" Shaved on one side and currently dyed a vivid green, I didn't see her point.

Dina chose a short plaid skirt with a cream-col-ored top that barely touched the waistband. Any shorter and the principal would have sent her home to change. Under that mini, thong panties that looked massively uncomfortable seeing as how her ass crack ate the fabric. Her dark hair hung straight and shiny, not one strand out of place.

Frieda marked the day with a clean pair of track pants and matching hoodie. She favored comfort above all else. As for her hair? A messy pixie cut, not by choice. She'd neglected brushing her hair during the March break, and the knots proved im-possible to remove. A trip to the hairdresser left her with a more manageable style.

Given we lived only a mile from school and

Mom claimed the fresh air did us good, we walked. Not together, I should add. While we shared a converted attic-loft bedroom and were close—like duh, we did share a womb, after all—when it came to social circles, we each had our own set of friends. We split up as we exited the house, knowing we'd hang later when we celebrated with Mother at a restaurant.

For me, my school day started under the bleachers with my best friend, Maya, and a joint. First period was history—boring. Then government—even more boring. By the time I finished science, my buzz wore off. Just in time for lunch, whereupon I got high again.

As I toked on the skunky joint, I eyed the moon creeping across the sky. "What time's the eclipse supposed to happen?" I asked, squinting at the sun's brightness.

Maya shrugged. "Sometime during last period. Apparently, Mr. Gruber got us some glasses so we can watch it." Mr. Gruber being our English teacher.

"Cool." It actually was. Sixteenth birthday, Friday the 13th, and an eclipse? Like, holy shit. I just hoped I got to see it. My cramping stomach had been getting worse all day. Could it be the elusive period my sisters and I had yet to get? Just in case, before the tardy bell rang, I hit a bathroom

3

and slid a pad into my underpants. Mom had been insisting for years we have some stashed in our lockers because she believed in being prepared. For once, I might not call her crazy.

The discomfort intensified as the afternoon went on, enough I almost asked to be excused, but the buzz of excitement over the upcoming eclipse kept my ass in my seat rather than skipping.

Last period, as promised, Mr. Gruber handed out the special glasses and we headed outside. It seemed like all the classes did, given the number of students milling on the football field. The groundskeeper had to be gnashing his teeth, seeing his immaculate turf being trampled.

I spotted my popular sister, Dina, by the team benches with her gaggle of posh girlfriends, holding court and flirting with a good chunk of the football team. Frieda sat in the bleachers, face buried in a book. Apart from us, she preferred her own company.

Given we had a few minutes until the big event, I tried to slip away, wanting to smoke the half-doobie I had left, only I got corralled by the stern vice principal, the steely-eyed Mrs. Transom. She took one look at me and pointed to my class. Detention sucked. Don't ask how I know. I sulked back to my group.

It wasn't so horrible. As the moon neared the

sun, strange wavy lines appeared on the ground. Kind of cool and hypnotic. I found myself watching them as our teacher droned.

"...what you're seeing are shadow bands, a prelude to the eclipse, which means time to put on the glasses and keep them on, especially when looking at the disappearing sun. We don't want anyone going blind."

That warning was enough for me to jam the ugly things on my face. The things Mr. Gruber called shadow bands rippled oddly when seen through the lenses. More annoying, my exposed skin itched then began to burn even as my flesh remained unmarked. No one else appeared to be uncomfortable, so I gritted my teeth and tilted my head back. The edges of the sun appeared to pulse as the moon began to cover it.

My stomach wrenched hard enough I bit my lip lest I cry out in pain. Fuck me, if this was my period, it could screw right off.

The moon hit the halfway mark on the sun, and my vision blurred. Were the glasses not working? I blinked and could see spots of light behind my lids.

What's happening?

A question not asked by me. I'd have sworn I heard my sister Frieda inside my head. Obviously, my mind was playing tricks. I opened my eyes and glanced at the bleachers to see Frieda standing, one hand dangling by her side holding the book, the other on her stomach as if she, too, cramped. Don't tell me we were going to pull some triplet bullshit and all go on the rag at the same time?

A peek over at Dina showed her trying to shove her way through the group of boys, a smile pasted to her lips, but I knew her well enough to see something bothered her.

Without even thinking of it, I moved for my sisters as the sky darkened. The world around lost all color. All shape. Even sounds became a blur. All I could see were my sisters. The three of us converged, reaching for each other, looking for comfort, hands clasping and forming a circle just as the full eclipse hit.

Pure blackness fell.

I could see nothing.

Hear nothing.

Feel nothing.

Until a single chime sounded and a bright, pinkish light flashed before my eyes. A voice, dulcet and soft, yet, at the same time, a booming vibrato, shook me as it said, "*It is done. The promise has been fulfilled.*"

What was done?

A second later, pain ripped through me, a pain so intense I wanted to scream, but not a sound emerged. Only agony existed. I hit the ground on my knees. The extreme torment might have torn me apart if not for the anchoring strength of my sisters. We still clung to each other, hands linked, the suffering shared.

By the time light returned, the sun no longer hidden by the eclipse, I found myself tense and panting. The discomfort vanished.

I blinked at my sisters and wondered if my expression matched their pale ones.

A trembling Frieda surprised me when she said, "What the fuck just happened?"

For once, I didn't have a smart-ass reply.

As Dina stood, I noticed red liquid rolling down her bare legs. "I think you got your period," I stated, only to realize I felt a warm wetness in my own crotch.

Frieda murmured, "And so it begins."

Happy fucking birthday, and the one that changed the course of our lives.

1

·)·)·)·⟨◉⟩·(·(·(·

THE PRESENT.

THE APARTMENT STANK OF WEED, body odor, and rotting take-out. Not surprising given the scumbag who lived here, one Theodore Gallant, currently out on bail for aggravated assault, rape times two, and illegal possession of a firearm. Back in the day, the scumbag would have been kept behind bars until his trial. Alas, in these modern times, criminals had more rights because, don't you know, it wasn't their fault. It wasn't the scumbag's fault he beat up Pamela Lorenz. He'd had a tough childhood. It wasn't his fault he raped her so violently she spent two weeks in critical care. His

9

mother never hugged him enough. As for the firearm? How was he supposed to know the guy who sold it to him from the trunk of a car in an alley did something illegal?

Theodore "Scumbag" Gallant presented a classic case of wasted space on this Earth, and yet he currently walked free, while his victim lived in a state of fear, refusing to leave her room and only having contact with her mother.

Enter me, who hated scumbags. When Mrs. Lorenz approached me—not directly, of course, as I never meet my clients in person and relied only on the dark web for communication—I took the job for much less than my usual fee. Some things you just had to do for pleasure... and justice.

The door to the shithole opened and in staggered Gallant. I should add, he didn't stumble because he'd gotten drunk. His unsteady step came from the weight of the woman draped limply over his shoulder. His unconscious date had a bit of meat to her bones, and I doubted she'd given consent.

It appeared I'd chosen the right night to pay Theodore a visit.

It took him a moment to notice me. First, he dumped the unconscious woman onto his couch. Then he muttered, "Fucking heifer."

"Well, that's rude," I replied, the words dropping starkly in the silence.

Theodore whirled so fast he almost fell over. His eyes widened as he took me in before he blurted out, "Who da fuck are you? Why are you in my fucking place?"

"Why don't we start with what the fuck do you think you're doing with her?" I gestured to the woman drooling on the nasty couch cushion. You couldn't pay me enough to sit on any fabric in this place. Heck, I'd wiped down the wooden chair before parking my ass in it.

"What I do is none of your fucking business. So get out unless you want to join in." He licked his lips as he grabbed his crotch. There didn't exist a universe where it would have been sexy. No wonder he relied on drugging his dates.

"If I wanted a skinny two-inch dick, I'd finger myself."

The insult had him snarling, "Fucking whore, we'll see how small you think it is when I choke you with it!"

"You and what army, dickwad?" I stood, and as often happened, the bravado began to wither from my target as he faced someone as tall as him at six feet. I'd hit a growth spurt after my sixteenth that didn't stop until my early twenties. Annoying, seeing as how I had to special order my pants so my ankles didn't show.

"Mouthy bitch. We'll see how brave you are once you meet my sharp friend." He pulled a puny blade, the metal of it marred in orange and brown streaks.

I grimaced. "When was the last time you cleaned that thing?" Good thing I kept up to date on my tetanus shots.

Rather than reply, he jabbed it in my direction. Easy to sidestep. I chopped his hand hard enough he yelped and dropped the knife. Before he could recover, I'd grabbed hold of his greasy hair, and he uttered a fitting pig-like squeal.

He didn't yip for long. I wrapped my arm around his neck and squeezed, making him claw at my leather sleeve to no avail. I bought quality shit because, in my line of work, every layer of protection helped.

My grip remained tight as I dragged his ass to the already cracked window, the sill of it showing burn marks and ash. A wobbly table sat to the side of it with drug paraphernalia strewn across it: crack pipe, needles—that I steered clear of—empty baggies, an ashtray full of roaches. Me, I preferred the cleaner high from a bong or vape pen.

Scumbag twisted and pulled as I heaved the window into its widest position. The night air rushed into the large opening, the screen that might have once protected from accidents long gone. Three stories up. Enough to kill a man—especially if he landed headfirst.

Without a goodbye speech—because, quite honestly, Scumbag here knew his crimes and I had no interest in listening to him lie about how he could change—I tossed him out. He didn't make a sound unless the splat counted. I tossed his crack pipe out after him. Make it look like an accident and the cops wouldn't dig deeper. Why would they? One less crook in the system made their lives easier. It would be one less predator to take up resources and court time. Even better, there would be one less victim, not that the snoring woman on the couch would ever know. She'd slept through it all.

Job done. Time to leave before I got noticed. Usually, the cops took their sweet time answering calls in this part of the city, but a body in the alley would garner a more rapid response.

As I headed for the door, I paused. If I left the woman behind, who knew what might happen. The cops weren't the only danger around. Predators thrived preying on the weak.

You're not a hero. A reminder that I'd not come here to save anyone, just to collect the paycheck at the end. Still... I also wasn't an asshole.

With a sigh, I grabbed the woman in a fireman

hold, slung her ass over my shoulder, and exited. People might see, but none would talk. This kind of place didn't encourage snitching.

I carried the girl to an apartment on the first floor, currently empty of people, the bathroom torn apart to fix some plumbing. A safe place for the woman to wake up, realize her poor life choices, and get her ass home in one piece. To those who thought me cruel to leave her instead of bringing her home, I drew the line at being a taxi service for idiots who drank too much with strangers.

I'd been that idiot in college. Woken up beside more than a few regrets. Did I blame those guys for taking advantage? Well, yeah, but I also took responsibility for the fact I'd behaved stupidly. I owned my actions, even the ones that made me look—and feel—bad.

With the girl more or less secured, I left, my steps quick, my face shrouded by the hoodie I wore under my leather jacket. No mask for me. That kind of shit drew more attention now that the pandemic was long past.

Once I returned home—three subway switches and a ten-minute walk later—I sent a message to my client: *Done.*

Within the hour—the length of time it probably took my client to verify my claim—my crypto account received payment and I went looking for my next job. Lucky me, an assassin for hire never lacked for work.

My plans to line up my next gig ended up derailed by a knock at the door.

I yelled, "Not now, Frieda." I didn't have to tune into the doorbell camera to know who stood on the other side. Ever since our sixteenth birthday, my sisters and I had been more closely attuned. By that, I meant we could feel each other's more extreme emotions—which made for awkwardness after a night of good sex. Poor Frieda, the almost virgin of the group, had a hard time meeting my or Dina's gaze the mornings after.

Since our sixteenth, we could always find each other, too. Like homing pigeons, we'd never be lost. Which led to the more annoying part of our curse: the inability to stay far apart for long. And not for a lack of trying. We'd not realized the issue until Dina wanted to go to a summer camp out of state. Within days, she became violently ill and returned within the week. Even vacations failed. Either we all went, or we planned really short excursions.

Given this quirk, we ended up buying a derelict three-story brownstone and renovated it into three large apartments, one sister per floor. Close yet private. We loved each other, but sometimes a woman needed her own space.

Frieda didn't knock again. She didn't have to.

15

While I wanted nothing more than to relax and do fuck all but browse the web, I couldn't avoid my sister. She wouldn't be bothering me without cause. Frieda hated leaving her place. The problem with seeing the future? Turning it off every time she set foot outside. I bugged her that she needed to practice more, but she never listened.

She brought with her a portent, a sensation that tingled the skin and let me know shit was about to happen. Heck, shit had been happening since our sixteenth birthday.

The day we got our powers.

2

THE PAST.

Back to the day of the eclipse, our red flood, and a sixteenth birthday gone off the rails...

"THIS IS BULLSHIT," I muttered while pacing the bedroom I shared with my siblings.

My sisters and I had fled the football field—with our bleeding uteruses—as quickly as we could bolt. Thankfully no one noticed the blood rolling down Dina's legs or the wet spot on Frieda's dark pants. My pad saved me from embarrassment, but it wouldn't contain the gush for long. The moment we arrived home, we rushed to strip out of our soiled clothing. We let Dina shower first, and then I motioned for Frieda to go next. The pad I'd put in place had already been swapped out for a fresh one.

When my turn came, I grimaced at the pink water swirling down the drain. Nasty but at least the cramping had calmed down. Guess I could now officially call myself a woman.

With a fluffy towel cinched around my boobs and body, I emerged fresh and clean to find grave expressions on my sisters' faces.

"What's got you so glum? It's just a period," I scoffed. Unpleasant, to be sure, but not entirely unexpected.

"Is it just that?" Dina arched a brow. *Or haven't you noticed something different?*

It took me a second to realize Dina's lips hadn't moved with the second question. Yet I'd heard her.

"Cool ventriloquist trick. I didn't know you'd been practicing," I stated, heading for my dresser and some clean clothes. I dropped the towel on the way, nudity with my sisters not a big deal. After all, we shared the same genetics.

"She's got it too," Frieda's quiet comment.

"Got what?" I tossed over my shoulder as I snared underpants and a T-shirt.

"Take a look in the mirror."

I grimaced at Dina. "A look at what? Is this your way of saying I'm bloated? Because duh, they taught us it was normal in health class." Just like the cramps should be expected.

"Oh, for fuck's sake," Frieda huffed. She whirled around and lifted her shirt, showing off a tattoo on her back. A series of symbols running up from the crack of her ass to just below mid-spine. Done in white, not black. Odd choice.

"Damn, when did you get that done? Has Mom seen it?" I exclaimed, kind of jealous. I'd always assumed I'd be the first one to get a tat.

"It appeared today." Frieda lowered her shirt as Dina lifted hers and murmured, "Ditto for me."

I blinked at the similar markings in my sisters' flesh. "Wait, you guys got tattoos without me?"

"No, dummy. I'm saying they just appeared. You've got one too."

"Bullshit," I exclaimed, yanking on my underpants. "I can't believe you left me out."

"Oh, for Christ's sake, look in the mirror." Dina repeated the order.

"Don't see why. Think I'd know if I got a tat," I muttered as I marched to the full-length mirror bolted to the back of our door. As I got close, I whirled and glanced over my shoulder, ready to unleash on my sisters, only to slam my mouth shut hard enough my teeth clacked. I blinked, and yet that didn't make the markings down my spine disappear.

"What the ever-loving fuck?" I breathed. "How did this happen?"

"I don't know," my book-loving sister stated unhappily. "But I suspect the eclipse played a part."

"Don't be ridiculous," I scoffed. "Eclipses don't give people tattoos."

"Then how do you explain it?" Frieda insisted.

"Explain what?" Mom entered at that moment, a woman beautiful for her age, which she wouldn't reveal for some crazy reason. We had her pegged at between mid-thirties to early fifties. Hard to tell given her smooth features and hair unmarked by gray. The woman never celebrated a birthday, which I found odd given she always made a big deal about ours.

I plastered my hands over my boobs, glad that I at least had underwear on. "Mom! You're supposed to knock."

"Don't be a prude, Enyo. I gave birth to you and wiped your ass. Not to mention, I have the same body parts."

"It's called respecting our privacy, Mother," Dina snottily replied. "We're young ladies now."

Mom snorted. "You're children living under my roof, and you're currently avoiding what's got you in a tizzy."

"We got our periods," Frieda blurted out. The

weak link in our triplet chain. She never could keep a secret from Mom.

The statement arched Mother's brow. "All three of you?"

"During the eclipse," Frieda added without any kind of prodding at all. I usually liked to hold out for a treat, like Mom's chocolate brownies.

"Is the start of your menses the only thing that's happened?" Mother asked, her laser stare fixing me in place.

"Isn't that enough?" was my sarcastic retort.

"Do you feel different? Has something about you changed?" Mom prodded.

Fuck it. Rather than speak, I whirled to show her my tattoo.

"Do you all have the mark?" A strange thing to ask. Most parents would have lost their shit at their child getting inked.

As my sisters showed off their tattoos, I tugged a shirt over my head. Mom might have birthed me, but as a teen girl with boobs that had been changing, I'd yet to get comfortable in my new skin.

"I swear we didn't go behind your back and get them." Frieda immediately begged for mercy. As if Mom would punish us for something like that. She had her share of ink on her body. Most of it symbols that she told us she'd explain when we got old enough to understand.

"They just appeared," Dina added. "We didn't have them this morning."

"It's finally happened. I wondered if it would," was Mother's cryptic reply.

"Why don't you seem surprised?" I questioned, because nothing about this day made sense, not even her response.

"I always knew you were special. Just look at the moment of your birth. Do you know how rare it is to have a child born under an eclipse? I wasn't due for a few more weeks, but the labor hit me so fast I had you on the side of the road under the eclipse's dark light."

We'd heard this story before. "We know. You popped us out one, two, three, like candy in a Pez dispenser, and all before the eclipse ended." A wonder we'd all survived. By the time the ambulance arrived, Mom had the cords cut and our newborn butts swaddled.

Mom nodded despite my levity about our birth. "A miracle birth on an auspicious day, at a rare moment. I wondered if you would be destined for great things. I believe we got our answer."

"Answer? How are spontaneous periods and tattoos an answer?" I blurted out.

Dina proved calmer. "You expected something like this to happen."

Mom nodded.

"And didn't warn us?" I couldn't keep my mouth shut.

"Warn you about something that might never happen?" Mom shrugged. "I had no idea if you'd be blessed."

"Blessed how? I'm bleeding like a stuck pig, crampy, craving chocolate and salt, and have a tattoo on my back I didn't ask for. And to which I'll add, wasn't what I'd have chosen." I'd been eyeing a thorned bicep vine for my first when I turned eighteen.

A hand wave from my mom didn't ease my annoyance. "Take some Tylenol for the discomfort. The menses part can be eased in the future with a blend of herbs. And if you're hungry, then, by all means, raid the pantry."

I scowled, but before I could blast my mom, quiet Frieda spoke. "What do you mean when you say we're destined for great things?"

"Only time will tell. In the meantime, you'll have to prepare. I'll have to make some calls so we can get started right away."

"Calls to who? Prepare for what?" Dina frowned, a rarity, as my perfect sibling worried even at her age about wrinkles.

"Those who can teach you the things I can't." Mom clasped her hands and beamed. "I can't wait for you to begin your training."

"What kind of training?" My suspicious query.

"That will depend on the results of the tests."

I rubbed my forehead and let Frieda tentatively ask, "What kind of tests?"

Mother's smile held no hint of humor or sarcasm as she declared, "Those to discern what kind of magic you wield."

As a sixteen-year-old, I did the most normal thing.

I laughed.

Until I saw the proof.

3

THE PRESENT.

I CAN WAIT ALL DAY.

Despite all my mental shielding, Frieda had the ability to make me hear her whether I wanted to or not.

Must I? I groused as I trudged to the door. We both knew I'd let her in eventually. While we might snarl and snap—the result of being too close, if that makes any sense—we never turned each other away.

I disarmed my alarm system then undid the locks on my reinforced steel door. To those who might think it excessive, remember I killed people for a living. I expected to have enemies. What I didn't want was to be caught unaware because of a flimsy lock and a door easily kicked in. My sisters' security proved even more intense, as I wouldn't see them harmed for things I'd done. Dina's dog might be cute and cuddly with her and tolerant of me and Frieda, but it would tear the arm off anyone else who entered without permission. Frieda's floor held a safe room that would protect her if she panicked and needed a place that wouldn't trigger any glimpses of the future. Think of a Faraday box, but for a magic-wielding human. I'd paid a pretty penny for that installation.

The heavy portal swung open, and Frieda entered wearing a loose ankle-length skirt of bright blue layered with a bulky mustard-yellow sweater. Her feet remained bare. A hater of shoes and socks, she only wore them when she left the building, which didn't happen often. As time passed, my sister became more and more of a hermit. At times, Dina and I worried about her mental health, which didn't go unnoticed, as Frieda read our minds and told us to fuck off, insisting she was fine.

"What's wrong?" I asked, heading for the fridge and a beer. Nothing like sucking on a cold glass bottle to soothe.

Without preamble, she blurted out, "You have to say no."

Head stuck in the fridge, I frowned, not at the

statement but at the fact I'd drunk most of the two-four bought only a few days ago. No getting drunk tonight unless I cracked the bottle of rye in my cabinet.

"Don't you dare drink the rye. It makes you fire off your gun randomly, and right now you need to listen."

Ugh. I grabbed one of the three remaining beers and didn't offer one to my sis. She didn't drink. I slammed the fridge door shut before replying, "What am I saying no to?"

"You're going to get an incredibly generous offer."

"Oh really?" I'll admit, intrigue replaced my annoyance.

"Yes really, but you need to refuse."

That statement arched my brow as I smacked the lid of the bottle off the stone countertop. It popped and plinked into the bin I kept underneath for exactly that reason. A bin almost full. "Why would I say no to this deal if it's incredible?"

"Because you have to," Frieda insisted.

A hearty swig went down, the dark ale frothy and delicious, before I asked, "Why? Am I going to die if I say yes?"

"Possibly."

"Get maimed?"

"Likely."

"Sounds like a fun time."

"I'm being serious, Enyo. You have to refuse."

"Why? What aren't you telling me?" I hounded my sister. "Will you, or anyone I actually like, die or be hurt? Will our house burn down? Will the government suddenly take an interest and lock our asses up for testing?" Probably my biggest fear.

"I don't know. Maybe."

"You're going to have to do better than that if you don't want me to say yes."

"How about because I said so?" Frieda huffed.

"Not good enough," I replied as I took another swig. It should be noted Frieda often freaked out. Part of the whole "seeing multiple futures" thing. She saw the potential of what could happen, and it scared her so much that she rarely left the house. It led to her having no real friends apart from me and Dina. Heck, she'd almost remained a virgin, considering she knew ahead of time whether or not sex would be good—and if the relationship would work out. Not well, as it turned out, since she also couldn't help but see how each partner would die —and none of them could be saved. Rather than deal with a future that sucked, she avoided it. Avoided life. Not just her life, though. She often meddled in ours.

Personally, I didn't want to know what to expect unless it resulted in something really, really bad. Otherwise, I liked surprises.

My refusal to obey pinched Frieda's lips. "You don't understand. He's going to take you away."

"He who? Who's taking me away?" Her claim made no sense.

"The Warden."

The name lifted the corner of my mouth. "Now there's a supervillain name if I ever heard one."

"He's not a villain," she muttered.

"And yet, he's going to try and kidnap me. Guess he'll be in for a surprise when I turn around and show him why that's a bad idea."

"You're not taking me seriously," Frieda huffed. "You have to listen. The Warden is going to make you an offer so incredible you'll be tempted to accept. But you can't because, if you do, everything changes."

"Changes how?" More than two decades of my sister freaking out had led to me being a little less accepting of her demands. Because of her, I'd missed out on prom—she'd claimed something bad would happen. I later found out that by "bad," she meant I'd have a drink spilled on me. At the college we attended together, she cock-blocked me at every turn, spouting things like this dude and that guy wouldn't respect me. As if I cared about respect when I was horny. She had me turn down jobs because there existed a single future out of many where I got injured. Kind of a given in my line of work. Over time, the bubble-wrapping of my feelings got to be cloying, hence why I stopped listening unless death or grievous maiming was involved.

"That's the problem. I can't fully see what lies ahead."

That brought a frown. Usually, Frieda couldn't see when things affected her, which could only mean, "You're going to be drawn into this job somehow." Being a terrible sister, I laughed. "Holy shit, you might actually have to leave the building for once."

"This isn't funny. I don't want to be involved in whatever it is the Warden wants from you. You know I can't do what you do." She waved a hand.

My lips quirked. "You can say it. I kill assholes."

"You execute people for money."

"Don't knock it. It's very lucrative," I said, taking another swig of my ale. My gigs had paid for the bulk of the building and repairs, while Dina covered the rest. Frieda, who couldn't hold down a job or tolerate leaving the apartment for any period of time, relied on us for her needs. Not something we usually minded, but I did have to draw a few lines for my own sanity. One of them being I decided which jobs I took.

"We have enough money in the bank," Frieda argued.

"I disagree." I had my eye on a place in Texas by the ocean that, with a little investment, would give us a second home. If we could convince Frieda to travel. At times, I hated the bond between us. When it came to travelling any distance, we couldn't go more than a few days without contact before the discomfort became too great.

What I wouldn't kill to get a week—fuck it, a month—alone on a tropical island with a lovely cabana man and room service.

"What are we disagreeing about?" Dina swept in without knocking or using a key. Stupid powers. She got to be the witch of the group, using magic to infuse her special potions, which she turned around and sold for a pretty penny. Not her only trick. She also used her power of persuasion to get people to do her bidding. Dina had come in really handy when we had to float my very heavy exercise system from the street to the basement level where we had a sound—and fire—proof training room set up.

"Frieda wants me to turn down a job that's going to pay big bucks." My quick explanation before I finished off my beer.

"How many dollars?" Dina's first question.

I shrugged. "No idea. Hasn't happened yet."

Dina glanced at Frieda, who muttered, "He's going to give her something priceless."

"Sweet," I chirped.

"Is someone going to die if Enyo accepts?" Dina's next query.

I pushed away from the counter as I answered. "She has no idea. She's being pissy about it because it might end up involving her."

At that, Dina rolled her eyes and uttered a dramatic, "Oh no. You might have to do something. However will you survive?"

"Not funny," Frieda gritted out. "I've got a weird feeling about this job."

"It's called anxiety because you've not set foot outside of this building in over three months." I'd been keeping track because Frieda's reluctance had been getting worse.

"I went outside a few days ago," Frieda argued.

"The front step to grab a package doesn't count," Dina retorted. "It's not healthy for you to stay inside this much."

"I go onto the roof almost daily for fresh air." Frieda tried to defend her actions.

I wasn't having it. "That's not a life, and you know it. Why are you so afraid to leave?"

Asked and yet I knew the answer before Frieda murmured, "Because I can't help them."

By them, she meant the people she encountered whose futures she could see. Most would live long lives that, while not always happy, were normal. Others, Frieda could see the ugly that would come. Most of it not preventable. She'd tried.

The first time she perceived the future was for our neighbor, Mrs. Kowalski, not even a week after our sixteenth. Frieda saw her getting hit by a bus while chasing her dog who'd escaped the yard. So Frieda asked to borrow the dog before it could happen. She returned the pup later that day to find an ambulance in front of Mrs. Kowalski's place. She'd been in her garden when a car with a drunken driver left the road, rammed through the fence, and killed her.

Total *Final Destination* shit. And Frieda's first introduction to the fact some futures were actually set in stone. But not all. Sometimes she would see a fork in the road or even a few branches. Her guidance had helped me on many a mission when I first started out as a killer for hire.

Or as Mother called me, once she discerned my ability, assassin. While one sister saw the future and the other wielded magic, I became the muscle of our trio.

Super strength. Speed. And an ability to fight like a superhero, only without the cape, tights, cool name, or flying power. Which I didn't mind, seeing as how I rocked the leather biker-chick look.

"You can't hide inside forever," Dina said softly to our sister.

"Easy for you to say. You don't see what I do." Frieda's voice cracked before she caught herself.

"Maybe you should try those relaxation exercises Mom taught you."

"They don't work," Frieda snapped.

"And neither do you," my blunt rebuttal. "Hence why, when it comes to jobs, you don't get a say."

Hurt twisted Frieda's features.

Guilt hit me fast and hard. "I'm sorry."

"No. You're right." Frieda's shoulders slumped. "I contribute nothing."

"That's not true. You warned me to stay far away from that dude with the genital herpes," Dina reminded.

"And kept me from getting my head blown off in that ambush at the docks." My client had actually been the father of someone I'd killed. He wanted revenge on me for eliminating his scumbag of a son. With Frieda's warning of thugs waiting to beat my ass to death, I'd adjusted my plan and taken them out from afar, my sniper skills coming in handy. Then I'd sent the grieving father to join his son—after he transferred the money owed for the job with a twenty percent tip for being a two-timing douchebag.

Frieda's lips remained turned down only for a moment before a wicked glint came into her gaze. "You know what, take the deal."

"Wait, what?" The sudden about-turn roused my suspicious side.

"It will be worth leaving the house to see you meet your match."

My brows drew together. "What's that supposed to mean?"

Her enigmatic smile went well with Frieda's bold statement. "You might want to think about shaving those Sasquatch legs above the knees is all I'm saying."

That comment dropped even Dina's jaw.

"Hold on, are you saying I'm going to fuck my new client?" I mean, I'd done it before. A hot dude was a hot dude. But why did she seem so amused by it?

"You're going to do more than that, dear sister. If my vision is right, you're going to fall in luuuuuve."

Like fuck. Me and relationships didn't get along. I wasn't built for love.

4

·)·)·)·⊕·(·(·(·

THE PAST.

THE WEEKS after our sixteenth birthday turned
out to be busy ones that involved many, many tests.
Some of them were so boring—like when Janice,
Mom's hippie friend, came over and chanted while
waving around incense—I fell asleep. Others had
me yodeling, "I'm not a pin cushion." Like, how
much blood did they need to draw? Although I did
get really good at pissing in a jar without getting
any on my hands.

Most likely I wouldn't have been so annoyed if
it hadn't turned out to be for naught. Whatever

Mom sought, I didn't have. Of the three, I turned out to be a dud.

Not so my sisters. One of the tests, which apparently worked to draw out magic, led to us discovering Dina could make sparks out of thin air and move small objects.

"A witch, how fantastic," Mother exclaimed, clapping her hands.

I'll admit to being jealous. After all, what little girl didn't dream of having power?

Frieda's gift turned out to be something entirely different, and it triggered at random. I remember her coming into the kitchen, wailing, "He's going to find his wife in bed with another man and kill them both before shooting himself." A rather detailed summary that proved to be true a week later, according to the news. A seer of the future, a gift that had Mom looking somber as she murmured, "This can be both a great and terrible ability. But I know you're strong enough to handle it." Words meant to be reassuring and yet left Frieda wide-eyed with anxiety.

I would have taken it from her if I could. At least then I'd have a special power.

Did it bother me I'd not developed any? Fuck yeah. How unfair. We shared the same DNA.

I sulked. and Mom noticed. She snapped her fingers. "Don't even start with that moping thing.

You have an ability. I know it. We just have to draw it out." Mother wouldn't be deterred.

It led to many sessions in the kitchen where she brewed noxious potions, handing them to me to chug, one after another.

After a particularly vile one, I'd squinted and growled, "It's like you want me to shit myself."

"Such language," she chided, flipping through a recipe book, not an old dusty tome like movies loved. She had a three-ring binder with laminated pages of the spells written in some language I didn't understand.

"And where did I learn it from?" Mom might be a lady most of the time, but when she got pissed, she swore like a sailor.

Her lips curved. "I don't know what you're talking about."

I snorted. "Of course you don't." As she opened the cupboards looking for jars, I couldn't help but feel dumb at not realizing before now that my mom was a witch. I'd always assumed her collection of herbs and recipes was for cooking and a bit of alchemy. She had a shop where she sold creams and fragrances, some of them quite playful in name. Rub the Tub for cellulite removal and Zit Git for acne removal. Had she been practicing witchcraft under our noses this entire time?

"How long have you been a Wiccan?" I blurted out.

Mom glanced at me over her shoulder. "A Wiccan is someone who pretends she's got power." Her lip curled. "I am a witch."

"Like Dina."

Once more her mouth pulled into a smile of sorts. "Not exactly like your sister. There are different kinds of magic. Mine tends to lean to the darker side."

I gaped. "You're a villain."

She arched a brow. "Good and evil depend on what side you're on."

My turn to smile. "Yours of course. Good guys are overrated."

Her laughter proved contagious, and I warmed at her praise. "You are so definitely my daughter."

The moment of levity didn't last, as I ruined it with a somber, "What if I didn't inherit anything?"

"Don't be foolish." She grabbed my chin to force me to meet her gaze. Her fierce expression held me, for I could see the love and also the sheer belief as she said, "You are special, Enyo.

I begged to differ. I'd never felt more boring in my life. So dispirited I took up a hobby I hated. Running. The only thing I got after my first period? Too much energy—and frustration. I needed to burn it off.

I jogged for hours without getting tired. Was that my superpower? The ability to run marathons? If so, it sucked, and I didn't tell my mother. Why would I? She was busy doing who knew what, but it involved workmen in our basement and her being gone for hours. When she was home, she was closeted in her bedroom making phone calls.

Almost exactly four weeks after my sixteenth birthday, the cramping started again, and my already foul mood grew worse. I snapped at everyone, including my sisters. Not only did I turn into a bitch, I craved chocolate. All the chocolate, which got to be ugly in a house with three PMSing girls.

Mom didn't bother trying to do any tests during shark week. Smart idea because I most likely would have snapped. We started again the day after the crimson tide stopped.

Rather than sucking on a potion, Mom asked to see my tattoo. I leaned over the counter, my shirt lifted, as she eyed it with a magnifying glass.

"Have you figured out the symbols yet?" I asked.

"No. It would help if I knew which god put it there."

"God?" I repeated with a smirk. "I didn't know you believed in one."

"There're dozens of them. Some quite obscure."

"How is this the first I'm hearing about them?"

"I've spoken of the various gods before, but you rolled your eyes and mostly didn't pay attention."

True. "Well, I'm listening now. Tell me about these gods."

"I'm not going into all the different ones. If you're curious, I have books."

"Do you have one in particular you like?"

"Apate, goddess of deceit, is whom I serve," Mom said as if it were the most normal thing in the world. "She gave me her blessing at a young age. I've been her servant since."

"What's a blessing do?"

"Gives me my magic." Mom twinkled her fingers, and they sparkled.

"Did she give Dina and Freida their powers?"

She shook her head. "No. Their ability doesn't come from her."

"Then who?"

She shrugged. "I'm still trying to find out. I've been asking around, but no one recognizes their markings. But there are theories."

"Such as?"

"The eclipse made me think it might be a moon god, or the goddess Luna, but we have samples of the markings they place upon their disciples, and none of yours match."

"Luna is a Greek god. What about the other

ones from other cultures? Like the Vikings or the Christians. Could—"

Mother violently shook her head. "They wouldn't dare. Not a child born of a servant of Apate."

"We're not just your kid, though. Maybe the tattoo god came from our father's side."

You'd have thought I punched my mother the way her mouth rounded at me mentioning he-who-shall-not-be-named, a.k.a. our unknown father.

She recovered quickly with a snippy, "The only thing that human gave me was an orgasm that took root."

Well, at least my father was human. But that said, what did that make my mother? As she turned from me, I couldn't help but eyeball her and ponder her origin. When asked previously, she'd always waved a hand and vaguely stated she'd emigrated from Greece. Nothing more. Nor did we have any family to ask. It was the Grae sisters—and mother—against the world.

"How old were you when you got knocked up?"

"Old enough to know what would happen when we slept together. And before you ask, I wanted to get pregnant. It's why I didn't bother with birth control."

"Ew, Mom!" That was a little too much info for a sixteen-year-old.

"Just letting you know you were wanted."

"By you, not him."

"He never knew," she said softly. And with that, she left the kitchen saying, "I have an appointment downtown. See you later."

She escaped, and I wanted to scream. Instead, I went for a run. Not quite sweating, not tiring either. I made it to the school and began running the track. Round and around, lost in my own world, when someone startled me. "Nice pace."

I stumbled and would have fallen without his hand to steady me. Him being Chad Lisgar. The hottest guy in school and a cliché. Captain of the football team. Six-foot-something of muscle. And supposedly a nice dude.

Who currently smiled at me. Wait, had he spoken?

"You okay?"

I pulled away from his touch and nodded. "Yeah. You just startled me."

"I didn't know you ran."

"I started not long ago."

His brows rose. "Then what I saw is even more impressive. You've got great rhythm."

"Uh, thanks?"

His lips curved wider. "Shall we run?"

Wait, did he mean together? I didn't know what to say. I might be sixteen, but I'd not done much more than kiss a few guys, most of them a little too slobbery for me to enjoy it much. Like, keep your tongue to yourself.

Why was I thinking of kissing in front of Chad? Shit, he waited for an answer. "Um, no. I'm done running. I'm going for a toke now." Oh my fucking god, had I just admitted I was a stoner in front of him?

"Mind if I join you?"

"Uh, sure." It almost came out a question as I led the way to my spot under the bleachers. The joint came out of my slim wallet, but before I could dig for a lighter, he held one lit for me.

I must have looked surprised because he said, "I'm not as much of a straight as people think."

I puffed the joint, getting it going before handing it over. He inhaled like a champ and didn't cough. So not lying when he claimed to not be a rookie.

We shared it back and forth, and I blamed the high for our conversation.

"You with someone?" he asked.

"Nah. You?"

He shook his head as smoke wreathed his face.

"I can't believe we've never talked before," he stated.

"We don't exactly run in the same crowds."

"We should. You're hot." He leaned close to me.

I closed the gap.

The kissing proved nice. Nice enough that when his hand slid under the hem of my shirt, I let him give me a grope. But I put the kibosh on how fast things moved when he tried to tug down the waistband of my pants.

"No, thanks. That's enough for today." I went to push away from him, but his arms tightened around me.

"Don't be a tease."

"Don't be an asshole. I said no."

He didn't like that answer. His face tightened. "I don't know why you're making a fuss. Everyone knows you rocker chicks are sluts."

"And jocks are dicks," I snarled as I shoved to get away from him.

Shoved hard enough he flew a few feet and hit the bleacher post. He smacked hard and fell to the ground, not moving.

Oh shit. Had I killed him?

Apparently not because he rose with huffing nostrils and a nasty gleam in his eyes. His lip curled. "So you like it rough. Let's go then."

He charged me, and I whirled to run, only to

have him tackle me. We hit the ground hard, him on top, crushing me into the ground.

My mouth filled with blood before the throb from the wound in my cheek started. I'd bitten it when my chin hit.

The fucker began dry-humping against me and laughed. He thought this was funny. Oh hell no.

I uttered an enraged cry, and I bucked, heaving him off me, and sprang to my feet. I was advancing on him, fists clenched, before he scrambled to stand and held out his fingers, beckoning. "You think you can take me?"

He mocked the fact I stood almost a foot shorter than him. I was on the petite side then, especially compared to him.

I didn't care. I swung—clumsily, I should add —and my balled fist bounced off the arm he raised to block.

He grunted. "You're stronger than you look. Let's see how strong." His fist shot out, but before it connected, I caught it.

Not just caught it, I held it with no effort.

He grunted. Swore. Shout out a leg to kick.

I released his hand and caught his foot, yanking it and flipping him onto his ass. I couldn't have said who was more surprised, but by this point, he was at least angrier.

With a roar of rage, he came at me again. I

dodged and danced to the side. Instinct moved my hand in a punch that connected. Something crunched, and he hit the ground, curling in the fetal position.

He came up whining, "You broke my nose." His complaint was nasally as he gushed blood.

"I'll break something else if you don't take your raping ass home."

"Uptight cunt," he muttered.

"What's that? You want me to publicly beat your ass? How would that look, captain of the team, to be taken down by a girl?"

He stomped off. The adrenaline that had been sustaining me gave way to the shakes. The trembles followed me all the way home. As I entered the kitchen, I found Mom waiting with a bag of frozen peas.

She held it out. "Put this on your face before it bruises."

"How did you know?" I asked, putting the coolness to my throbbing chin.

"Frieda."

That brought a scowl. "She knew I was going to be attacked and did nothing?"

"Don't blame her. She told me, and I said to let it happen."

"Why?" I wailed. "Why would you let him hurt me?"

She stared at me. "Seems to me you hurt him more. And in the process discovered your ability."

At her claim, I blinked. "I did?"

Mom smiled. "I should have known you'd be a warrior."

And thus began my lessons in combat and my first in a long string of failed relationships.

5

·)·))·)·⊙·((·((·

The present.

Despite Frieda's warnings, she couldn't tell me anything about this so-called Warden. Not the nature of his offer, exactly who he was, or why she thought I'd fall in love.

Me, in love. Ha. I'd yet to meet a man who could handle my ass, and I meant that quite literally. See, after my sixteenth birthday, while my sisters gained a modest inch, I shot up to six feet. Not exactly a dainty height for men. Sure, I could be light on my feet, but I'd never be delicate or simpering, which it seemed most males preferred.

It didn't help that I didn't have it in me to be

49

submissive. I didn't hide my strength, which led to me attracting shorter, beta-male types. Too many of them fetishized me. For example, one fuckwad said, *"You're like an Amazonian goddess in need of worship. Let me climb you."* Like, no. And why?

With alpha types, I got the "Can't you be more girly" bullshit. I'm sorry, tits and boobs should have been enough. Skirts annoyed me. As did bras with wires for that matter. Makeup was Dina's thing. I felt like a clown the few times I slathered it on.

Then there were the bully males who felt a need to dominate. To show me they were stronger. The boss. They couldn't stand it when I handily beat their asses. What can I say? I wasn't about to pretend to stroke their egos.

So who exactly was this Warden that Frieda teased would not only get into my pants but make my cynical ass fall in love? I couldn't wait to find out. But a few days passed and nothing happened. It was enough to send me out to kill more scum of the city. And before you whine about me being judge and executioner, someone had to do it. Some scum never learned. Our local cops played catch and release, allowing assholes to keep victimizing over and over. I put an end to it. Not everyone can be redeemed.

Callous? Have you met my mother? Who do you think taught me how to kill? Well, not entirely her alone. She hired a whole cadre of instructors who trained me in weapons, combat techniques, and even war strategy. When I asked her as a young girl exactly who I'd be fighting for, she'd shrugged. *"If your god never appears, then whoever you damn well please."*

She later taught me to monetize my mercenary skills while she passed her business on to Dina, who'd expanded the line of potions and creams while updating what she called "tacky titles."

And now, instead of finding my next job, I waited for my sister's prophecy to come true.

A night of killing with four hours of sleep followed by a shower didn't ease the edge of anticipation. It wouldn't be long now. I could feel it in my bones.

I'd just finished dressing in a dark gray bodysuit for a training session when my doorbell app went off. A glance at my screen showed the retreating back of a delivery man from a local chain. I wasn't expecting a package, and yet one sat on the step, out in the open, tempting porch pirates.

No matter how many I taught the error of their ways, new ones always took their place. Even if not mine, best to fetch the package, as it probably belonged to Frieda or Dina. I skipped down the steps and opened the main lobby door that gave access to the stairwell into our building. The innocuous package had no company markings to identify it, nothing but my name written in big black marker.

Ooh. A bomb? Body part? Something else?

Would lifting it set it off? The delivery guy hadn't taken any precautions. Could be someone watched and waited to remote detonate it. Since I didn't plan on having a hole blown in our building, I did the responsible thing and booted the box as hard as I could—which would have made a soccer coach cream his pants if he'd seen it. The box soared across the street and hit the building on the opposite side, bounced off, and landed on the ground.

No explosion. So most likely not a bomb. I trotted across the street and retrieved my slightly battered package. It didn't weigh all that much, nor did anything rattle as I jogged back to my building. I carried it inside but didn't take it to my apartment. I knew better than that.

Down to the basement I went, into a secure room where Dina practiced her more aggressive magic, a.k.a. the lobbing of fireballs and lightning. The lead-reinforced walls with concrete behind them could handle most blasts. Once more I tossed the box to the far end of the room, where it landed with barely a thud.

I really hoped someone hadn't decided to surprise me with baked goods because by now they'd be mush. I exited the chamber to grab a gas mask with built-in goggles, along with gloves and a spear. An assassin had to have equipment for all types of situations. The mask had been bought for a job but never used. Instead of poisoning my target with gas, I'd tainted his food.

The mask clung to my face and protected not just my lungs but my eyes. People often forgot that those seeing orbs could be susceptible to toxins. The moist membrane was similar to an open wound.

The gloves were an added precaution, despite the fact I chose to use the spear to actually open the package. Holding it extended, I used the sharp tip to slice through the tape holding the top flap shut.

Nothing happened.

I pried the edges open and, with my height, could see inside.

"What the fuck," I muttered.

Within the box sat a grayish-blue ball about the size of a fist. It sat perfectly in the center. Odd, given the way I'd treated the package. It should have rolled around. I used the spear to tilt the box onto its side. The ball didn't budge. I poked it with the spear next. The tip of it didn't depress the surface or even leave a scratch.

Even more intrigued, I neared enough to reach down and poke it with my gloved finger. The ball didn't budge.

Had someone glued it in place?

Once more I left and returned, this time with a knife, which I used to saw the cardboard away until only the ball remained, stuck to a small section of the massacred box. Its innocuousness taunted me.

Why had someone sent it? It had to be some kind of message. I peeled off my glove and poked the ball with the tip of my finger. To my surprise, it rolled free of the cardboard.

Hunh. Strange. With my bare hand, I plucked it from the floor and grimaced as the surface of it stuck to my hand. More concerning, the ball began to deflate and expand over my flesh, making it tingle.

Crap. Some kind of chemical agent. Before I could mind-yell to my sisters to bring a venom kit, a bright light flashed, and when I blinked, I found myself elsewhere.

And by elsewhere, I mean a jungle. A fucking jungle!

6

·)·)·)·⊙·(·(·(·

I DID HAVE A SLIGHT MOMENT OF PANIC because, for one, I'd been teleported, something I would have claimed impossible like a minute ago. I mean, Mom had certainly never mentioned it was a possibility.

Two, I had no idea where I'd landed, but I could tell it was far, far from my sisters. My tie to them stretched thin, and the nausea already gnawed at my stomach. They had to be panicking since I always warned them when I had to travel.

Third, I'd arrived without a weapon, which annoyed because I was pretty sure the leopard eyeing me from the branch of a nearby tree wouldn't be sheathing its claws when it pounced. Its green eyes fixed on me, and I knew better than to show fear.

Rule of the jungle—concrete or natural—never look weak. I lifted my lip in a silent snarl.

I'd swear its eyes crinkled as if amused. Less funny? The thing that suddenly landed on my head. A swipe at a furry body sent a horrific spider to the ground, where it flipped around and flashed fangs.

Fucking fangs and hairy legs. Oh hell no. Stomp. Squish.

"I hate spiders!" I muttered before I craned to look overhead, only to widen my eyes in horror at the sight of the massive webbing lacing the branches. The filmy mess shook as more of the little eight-legged bastards came rappelling down looking for revenge.

Like fuck. Part of my training had taught me to make a weapon out of anything I got a hold of. In this case, a branch. I pinata-d the shit out of the spiders, whacking them left and right while screaming. Probably what scared off the leopard because, by the time I'd beaten the arachnids, a glance at the tree showed the green-eyed furball gone.

Good. I had enough problems currently, given I remained stuck—and lost—in a jungle. I tossed my gummed-up branch for a fresh one before setting off, choosing a direction not quite at random. I caught a hint of smoke in the air. My sneakers weren't exactly ideal for the conditions, their soft soles no protection if I happened to step on something unpleasant. My outfit covered me, but the form-fitting spandex did little to ease the humidity clinging to the air.

I'd not gone far when a low-hanging tree branch disgorged a threat. A fat serpent fell down and wrapped around my midsection. I tore it free and tied it in a knot. Cartoonish? Yes, but without a knife for chopping, I had no other ideas. And, no, I wasn't about to tear it apart with my bare hands. Gross.

By the time I reached the fast-moving river, it felt like I was in an old-school Atari game called *Pitfall*. I actually glanced around at the vines to see if any of them could be used to swing across. Alas, those perfect types of swinging ropes existed only in Tarzan movies.

I could have chosen to follow the river downstream, only the smell of smoke definitely came from across. Add to that I could see a bushwhacked path on the other side. It might have been a game trail, but the footprint in the mud on the shore across from me indicated otherwise.

Before venturing into the rapid current, I went looking for some sturdy vines. I found enough to braid, thereby making my makeshift rope stronger and long enough to tie around a tree trunk. I tethered the other end to my wrist just in case the river tried to sweep me away.

As prepared as I could be, I stepped into the shallow part of the water, my running shoes slipping on the slick mud. My arms waved to maintain my balance. I kept them out and ready to waggle as I moved deeper into the current that pulled at my legs, rushing between my calves. I'd have sworn more than once that something wiggled against me, too. As I forded to the middle, the river rose to my boobs, and despite the relative warmth of the water, my nipples hardened.

Halfway there. My next step I felt my foot sliding, and I had to fight to remain upright.

And failed.

The strong rush of water swept me a few yards before my tether snapped taut. I held on to the rope with my unbound hand.

A noise drew my attention to the shore I'd left.

A shore with a leopard standing on it.

It eyed me then the vine. The fucker bit down and severed it before I could get my feet planted.

The water swept me, and I could do nothing but bob, just fleshy flotsam that took breaths every chance I got. When my body launched into the air as the river rocketed off the edge of a sharp drop, I had enough air to shriek, "Yeeha!"

Wait, you didn't think I was scared, did you? I'd

done worse wild water rapids, and this wasn't my first time going over a waterfall. I'd been banned from ever going to Niagara again because of my thrill-seeking ways.

Arms tucked to my side, legs firmly together as I plummeted, I closed my eyes and huffed out my nose before I hit the surface. The force of my entrance sank me, but not far enough to hit bottom. Since I'd gone in feet first, I simply had to kick and stroke upwards, the bright sky a beacon that I strained for.

I emerged into the air face first and took in a breath. That was fun. I stroked away from the churn caused by the falling water, moving into the calmer parts of the plunge pool before throwing myself on my back for a float. That had been more epic than the ride I took down Lava Falls, a trip taken more than a decade ago when we could still convince Frieda to leave the house.

My moment of relaxation didn't last, as an object bumped me. A log, at first glance, that bobbed past.

A log with slitted yellow eyes.

Fuck me, a croc or gator. I didn't have time to figure out which, given it veered around and headed for me.

Treading water didn't give me the best advantage in a fight with an aquatic beast. Still, I waited for it to draw close before acting. It went to lunge with its open maw lined in teeth and I dove under and to the side, bursting from the water to throw myself on its back.

The oversized reptile didn't like that one bit and rolled us. Over. And over.

I dug my fingers into its eyes, feeling the pop of membranes. It thrashed as it reacted and threw me clear. I swam rapidly for shore and trudged my soggy ass away from the water while the frothing behind me calmed.

The jungle oozed vitality, the proximity to moisture rendering everything lush and green with the occasional pops of color from vibrant blooms. Despite the beauty of the place, I chose to relocate because where there was one watery menace, there would be two or more.

I'd purposely emerged on the side of the river I'd been angling for before I got swept away. A glance at the sheer rocky cliff and waterfall didn't daunt. Rock climbing had been a part of my lessons as a teen, and I'd continued doing it as a hobby into adulthood.

It proved an easy ascent, with plenty of hand-holds. There were only a few attacks: more spiders, one hissing rat-like creature, and a nest of shrilly-shrieking birds that, judging by the bones around them, would have taken a bite if I'd not moved quickly away.

Upon reaching the top, I paused for a look back and took in the untamed, natural beauty. Nice place. Maybe I could convince my sisters to come for a visit once I escaped. I wondered how hard it would be to get a teleportation ball now that I knew they existed. Frieda wouldn't have a choice if she got whammied from her apartment to the jungle.

The faint hint of smoke from before once more tickled my nose, and I followed it, new whacking stick in hand. I evaded two pit traps lined in spikes, a trip wire that triggered a swinging log—also with jagged spines—two nets, and a bear trap. Although, with it being in the jungle, would it be more of a cat trap? Maybe set to catch that leopard that caused my mishap in the river?

The acrid stench of fire grew stronger as I made my way through the jungle. The culprit being a campfire set in the midst of a clearing. A spit erected over it had something meaty cooking, the outer skin of it crackling and dripping fat. My mouth watered. I'd not gotten a chance to eat before being transported.

As I stepped over the trip wire guarding the camp, my eyes tracked all movement. The birds flitting from branch to branch. The snake slithering away from the heated coals and burning wood. No sign of life, and yet I wasn't alone.

My sudden whirl and flung fist caught the person behind me by surprise but didn't put him on his ass.

The big dude only arched a brow as my hand connected with his midriff. Impressive. I'd been known to break things when I hit.

I had to tilt my head slightly to see his face. Dude was tall and good-looking despite his rugged square-faced scowl. His green eyes perused me—my clothes slightly ruined, my hair a soggy mess—before he uttered in a deep rumble, "You actually survived?" I could hear the disbelief.

It arched my brow and brought out my bitch. "Sorry to disappoint." Then, because I hated big dudes who thought they were so tough, I hooked my foot around his legs, shoved, and sent him toppling to the ground.

What I didn't expect? Reflexes fast enough to have me land atop him!

7

The Warden

THE WOMAN WHO LANDED ATOP HIM oomphed in surprise. Yes, she'd managed to take him down, but he wasn't going alone.

Her surprised gaze met his, and the man most knew as the Warden drawled, "Did you learn that move in assassin school?"

"Nah, that was from my wrestling coach. This next one I learned from my mother."

He didn't manage to completely avoid the knee she rammed into his groin. He gritted his jaw against the pain and wrapped his arms around her before she could flee. "Where are you going? We need to chat."

"Chat or something else?" she purred, grinding her groin against him.

He hated that he felt an answering stir. "Was whoring yourself also part of your lessons?"

"What kind of misogynistic crap is that? If I flirt with a hot dude, I'm a whore? I can see why you need to kidnap women for company." To his shock, with unexpected strength, she broke his hold and sprang to her feet.

"Impressive."

"I hear that a lot." Rather than flee, or even take a fighting stance, she sauntered to the fire pit and leaned in to sniff. "What's for dinner?"

The unexpected query had him reevaluating the woman. She'd been nothing but surprises since she'd arrived. He took his time rising and answering. "Wild hog. Vicious and ugly but delicious when cooked."

She cast him a glance over her shoulder. "Can't wait to taste it."

Her nonchalance had him leery. "Aren't you going to ask who I am?"

"I'd say that's obvious. You're 'the Warden.'" She offered him finger quotes.

His lips pursed. "You've heard of me?"

"In a sense. I was warned we were going to meet."

"By whom?" Because he'd told his plan to no one.

"Doesn't matter. Why have you had me summoned here?" She gestured to the jungle.

"To see if you're fit for a task."

"Wait, this whole teleportation jungle adventure was part of a job interview?" Her mouth rounded in astonishment only for a moment before she smirked. "Explains why you were disappointed. You thought I'd fail."

"I'll admit you turned out to be more resourceful than expected for someone Western-raised."

"Why, Ward. You say the sweetest things." She clasped her chest over her heart and rolled her eyes. "If it helps, when I first heard your title, I kind of expected someone more impressive. And wide. I mean, if movies taught me anything, it's that someone with the title of warden is gonna have a gut out to here." She mimed a thick belly.

The grimace couldn't be contained. "I'm not that kind of warden."

"Then what exactly are you?" She cocked her head. "Wizard? Was it you who sent that spell?"

"Actually, a friend fabricated it for me." The woman before him had been the fifth one to be called in such a fashion but the first to actually make it to his camp in one piece. One of them had died while the others were too gravely injured to continue.

"Nice dodging of the question. Not a wizard, then what are you, Ward?"

"My name is Bane." The truth emerged, and her lips curved.

"Hello, Bane. I'm Enyo, which I assume you already know."

"I do. As mentioned, I had you called here specifically."

"Now that I've passed your little test, what's the offer? I'm going to guess by the jungle scene that you want me to pull some kind of Indiana-Jones-type of mission where I retrieve something cool being held by some cursed place crawling with enemies."

Bane blinked. "No."

Her lips turned down. "Well, that sucks."

"Wait, you would have wanted a dangerous task of that sort?"

Her shoulders rolled as she offered a wry grin. "A little adrenalized adventure never hurt anyone, and who hasn't dreamed of finding treasure?"

He almost grinned. Unheard of. Especially given the dire circumstances. "Sorry, no treasure, but there is great peril."

"Who do you want me to kill?" She went right to the point.

"That's not entirely clear yet."

"Then how do you know they need to be dead?"

"Because the fate of the world depends on it." A cryptic reply for a difficult situation.

It led to her snorting. "Dude, you don't need to fake some kind of grand cause. Just tell me how much it pays because that's all I'm really concerned about."

"Name your price."

She arched a brow. "That's kind of risky on your part."

"Wealth won't matter if I'm not around to spend it."

Her lips quirked. "Valid point." She paused then added, "My sister told me to refuse your offer."

The statement brought a frown. "What does your sister know of my business?"

"Whatever her vision showed, which, according to her, wasn't much. She sees the future. Or at least possibilities of it. She told me to turn you down."

The creases on his brow deepened. When he'd come across Enyo the assassin, he'd not actually looked into her family, mostly because he'd not expected her to pass muster. Given she'd been raised in the mundane world, he found it hard to believe she'd have the right skills, yet here she stood.

"What else did your sister say?"

Her lips curved. "That you and I are going to become lovers."

An outrageous claim that had him laughing. "We will never be lovers."

Judging by her piqued expression, she didn't appreciate his certainty. "Frieda is rarely wrong."

"On this I can guarantee she is. I'm already sworn to another."

Surprise marked her features. "You're married?"

"In a sense." No need to mention it was to his position. The task of Warden was for life. A life that didn't lend itself to settling down with a wife and having a family. A hard lesson he'd never forget.

She cocked her head. "How old are you?"

"Why?"

"Curiosity."

"Forty-three."

"I'm almost forty." Her nose wrinkled. "Which I don't see as a big deal but to hear my sister Dina, you'd think we were going to suddenly turn into crotchety old maids."

"Now who's dodging questions? What else did your sister supposedly see?"

"Not much because whatever you're about to drag me into will involve her. And she never can see her own future. A hazard of being a seer."

"An assassin and a seer. Interesting family."

"You forgot my mom and sister, the witches."

And the surprises kept coming. Apparently, he'd really underestimated Enyo. Honestly, after the first four failures, he'd hardly expected this woman to pass the tests. He'd only even auditioned her on the advice of Lance, the same person who made the teleport ball for him. His friend had said, *"I know you were looking for a warrior, but I've heard of an assassin, one not trained in the guild yet she's never failed a mission."*

The reminder of Lance's words had him asking, "How come you never trained with the assassins guild?"

Her brow arched. "You mean the guild that rejected me?"

"They must have had their reasons."

"At sixteen, they considered me too old."

His turn to lift a brow. "You started training in your teens?"

"I was a late bloomer. Luckily, my mother knew some people who didn't mind teaching me."

He had to wonder if her unusual education was what helped her to survive the many small traps he'd contrived to test applicants.

"You've yet to name your price."

"Kind of hard to do when you haven't explained exactly what you expect of me. And don't pull the save-the-world schtick again. I want details."

"In less than a week, a rare alignment will happen, whereupon a door to an ancient prison could be opened."

"Let me guess, there's a big baddie behind that door."

"Very bad, apparently, and yet there are those who would try to release it."

"And you want me to kill those people."

"More or less. You must keep them from killing me and opening that door."

"Sweet. How many are we talking about? Do we have deets? Location, any data on their habits—"

He interrupted. "There are too many to hunt down. Ultimately, you just need to guard me from harm. Especially on the day of the alignment. My job is to keep the portal closed, yours is to prevent them from getting at me and forcing it open."

"A defensive position?" Her nose wrinkled. "Why not hire an army of mercenaries for the job? You do realize my skills are in stealthy assassinations."

"There is already a force guarding it. You would be the last line of defense if any broke through."

Her lips pursed. "Meaning I'd be facing the toughest and wiliest. I like a challenge."

And he liked the way she smiled a little too much. "Does this mean you accept?"

"There is still the matter of payment," she reminded.

"I told you, name your price."

He expected something outrageous. Instead, she played coy. "What's the most valuable thing you own?"

His mind flitted to the island with its castle, probably his most ostentatious possession. One that only belonged to him because of his position. Just like the wealth wasn't truly his but that of the Warden.

As he thought over the things he actually owned, it came to him that nothing he'd accumulated truly belonged to him but for one thing. And so he wryly said, "The only thing I have that's worth anything is my position."

"Surely you have something more valuable than your job?"

He shrugged. "Sorry to disappoint. Although I should add my position does give me access to wealth. Jewels. Weapons. Surely there's something in the vault that can be used as payment."

"You have a vault of treasure?"

At his nod, she beamed before saying, "Why didn't you say so? Very well, upon completing the job, you will let me take one thing from this trea-

sure vault. Anything I want. Do we have a deal?"
She held out her hand.

He didn't hesitate before clasping it and saying,
"Deal." The jolt that went between them sealed the
bargain.

8

⋅⟩⟩⋅⟩⋅☼⋅⟨⋅⟨⟨⋅

I DON'T KNOW WHAT POSSESSED ME TO
make a deal without even seeing this so-called treasure vault. Like, what if it was all junk? Or
empty? Or...

Who am I kidding? I would have still said yes.
Yes from the moment he claimed I'd help save the
world. While I could lie—and pass any detector
doing it—the part of me that would never admit it
aloud kind of creamed her panties at the idea of
being a hero. Although it should be added that the
creaming part might also have something to do
with the hunky Warden with the even sexier name,
Bane. Who the fuck named their kid after a villain?
Hold on, my mom did that with me and my sisters.
Don't let anyone tell you the Graeae sisters of Greek

73

tales were nice. They were evil, conniving, and ruth-less... just like us.

Would Bane live up to his name, too? A girl could hope, and even if he didn't, the whole situa-tion—wild and unpredictable, dangerous and un-known—ticked every single one of my happy boxes.

Adventure? Check.

Pitting my wits and skills against foes? Also check.

Getting to choose a prize at the end while also getting the unofficial title "savior of the world"? Name me one person who wouldn't want to be in my shoes. Er, boots. At least once I got back to my place and could change out of my exercise gear.

Possibly the only annoyance? The fact the big dude laughed when I told him we'd be lovers. It should be known I didn't fuck guys willy-nilly. I had standards, which he met. As tall as me, broader, and not in need of a paper bag for his face. He also didn't fall to my feet in worship the moment we met and had some wit when he spoke—not that I liked talking during the act. I'd been known to slap my hand over a mouth if a guy ruined the moment.

"Glad that's settled. Not that I had much of a choice. You're the only one who actually succeeded."

Way to remind me that I wasn't his first choice. "Gotta say it's pathetic that the people you screened couldn't handle a jaunt in the jungle." I'd survived worse, like the time my mom had me dropped in the Rockies with nothing but a pocketknife. I emerged with a bearskin cloak.

"I see they forgot to add braggart to your list of skills."

My lips tilted. "It's not bragging if it's true."

"We'll see about that." Bane headed for the fire pit and the roasting hunk of meat. My mouth watered even as my tummy churned, my distance from my sisters making itself felt. It led to me asking, "So where's your real camp?" Because this clearing had nothing but the fire. No tent or even a bedroll.

"My home is on an island, which also happens to be where you're needed. We'll be making our way to it after we've eaten. That is, if you're amenable to walking."

"Do I have a choice?" I didn't exactly see how else we'd get out of the jungle.

He rolled his shoulders. "Not really."

"What if I'd said no to your deal?" I further queried as I neared him and the spit.

He pulled out a ball from a pouch hanging at his hip, much like the one that had brought me here. "I'd have sent you home."

"Hold on, if you have a ball capable of sending me home, why do we have to walk?"

"Because where we're going can't be accessed by magic."

My brows rose. "Well, shit. The more I learn, the less I know."

"Blame the fact you didn't attend a guild. I'm getting the impression your education in the arcane of this world is restricted."

My turn to shrug. "My mom taught us what she could, but even she said the world was full of secrets and we didn't have time to learn them all."

"So what did you learn?"

"How to gut a person. Punch. Choke. Poison. Garrote. Knife throw." I ticked off my many accomplishments as he began carving our dinner. "Muay tai. Jujitsu. Boxing."

"Boxing?" He paused as he held out a hunk of steaming meat on a blade. "That's got to be one of the most useless ways to kill."

"True, but when it comes to getting into places, it's awesome. Tall chick beating the piss out of big thugs while wearing skimpy daisy dukes? For some reason, rich dudes who invite me back to their mansions think money will keep me from killing them." I paused before adding, "Wrong."

He shook his head, and I caught a hint of a smile. "You really have no remorse for what you do."

"Remorse would imply shame. I'm not

ashamed of what I do. I kill people. Bad people, mostly. But there have been some who might have been considered morally gray. Here's the thing, though. The truly good don't have people hiring expensive assassins to take them out."

"Interesting data point if true."

"Let me guess, you're the type who hems and haws about killing. Assuming you've actually taken any lives."

"I've eliminated my fair share."

"And were they all deserving?"

"Given they were trying to murder me at the time, totally." Said with a grin before he popped a hunk of meat into his mouth.

We filled our bellies, eating a good chunk of the carcass. When done, he tossed the remains into the forest for the animals to finish, and he put out the fire.

Then, without pronouncement, he took off into the jungle. I followed, admiring his taut ass clad in khaki cargo pants. I'd yet to discern what being Warden meant. What did he guard? He'd mentioned having to defend himself and killing in the process. Did that mean those muscles weren't just for show? Some guys knew how to build bulk but not how to use it. The knife at his hip seemed more utilitarian than for fighting, given he'd used it to carve hunks of meat for dinner. No gun. Or sword. His hiking boots didn't have soles thick enough for a hidden blade.

The pouch by his side where he'd pulled the teleportation balls from didn't seem big enough for much more than maybe a grenade or two. Yet...

"Were you the one who built those traps in the woods?"

"Yes."

"And you're telling me the other people you brought over failed to spot them?"

"Well, the first one never made it out of the river. Between the spider venom, snake bite, and then the plunge from the falls, he was in no shape to play with the gators."

"What made you choose him if he sucked so bad at surviving?"

"Would you believe he was the best the assassins guild had to offer?" he grumbled. "I had plenty to tell the guild master after his abject failure. Today's assassins are woefully underprepared for anything outside a city."

"My mom used to randomly abandon me in weird places. The most annoying one being the desert stint." My nose wrinkled. "Sand in unmentionable cracks for weeks afterwards. But I have to say, the scorpions didn't taste as bad as expected. Way better than cockroaches."

He gagged.

I smirked.

"What else did you learn that wasn't about killing?"

"Swimming. Rock climbing. Bear wrestling was super fun and comes in useful with gators, too," I slyly added.

"Is there anything you can't do?" His sarcastic rejoinder.

"Cook. Sew. And my idea of diplomacy is shaking the person disagreeing until they see my point of view."

A noise came out of him that had me slewing a gaze in his direction. He appeared to be almost choking.

"What about you? What skills does *the Warden*"—and yes, I gave it an inflection—"have?"

"I know about the arcane world."

"Bullshit. You didn't know about my sister, the seer, or my other sis, the witch."

"I never said I knew everyone involved in the arcane. Do you really think your sisters are the only ones with powers?"

"How many more are there?" I blurted out. Honestly, I'd not given it much thought, nor sought it out much. I stayed in our city, we all did, because of the curse that bound us. Not to mention, I kept busy with my jobs. In retrospect, maybe

I should have explored more of the magical aspect of our lives. Then again, how does one go about looking for magical shit when people did their best to hide it? My sisters and I certainly didn't go around advertising it. People assumed that Dina's creams and potions, while they made claims of curing this or doing that, had to do with blends of herbs, not magical infusions.

As for Frieda, she didn't talk to many outside our little bubble. And she certainly never shared the knowledge of her gift with anyone. It led to annoying twats like that one friend she had in college, Santana something or other. Frieda made the mistake of telling her, and the next thing my sis knew, Santana was bugging her to tell her the future constantly.

"Who's my husband going to be? How many kids? What's on our test next week? What's the winning jackpot numbers?" When Frieda tried to explain her gift didn't work that way, Santana got mean. When she failed a midterm, but Frieda aced it, the jealous cow went to the professor and told them Frieda cheated. Then she stole the one boy Frieda had a crush on, which broke her heart. It didn't help my sister knew it was a possibility.

Frieda had sobbed on my shoulder. *"If he'd said no to her, he was going to be my first."* But that weak-dicked asshole broke her heart instead. As if that weren't enough, Santana got Frieda expelled, claiming my sister harassed her. That was the last straw. I didn't kill Santana, only because I knew Frieda would be upset, but that didn't stop me from posting the pictures of her blowing the college dean.

I'd almost lost my train of thought when Bane replied, "There are thousands of arcane around the world. Most human appearing, but not all."

I blinked. "Wait, what? You mean there really are monsters?"

"Monster is what humans call that which they don't understand."

"What do you call them?"

"Some are my friends."

I might have asked more questions, but the jungle suddenly went quiet. Noticeable given that up until now we'd been accompanied by the buzz of insects, the creak of branches, and the sway of leaves as animals passed through.

When everything ceased, so did my steps. Bane halted as well, and he closed his eyes as he lifted his head and turned it left, then right, his nostrils flaring as if he scented the air.

Rather than speak, he held up his hand, five fingers spread, a quick fist then four more fingers.

Nine opponents.

And what did he do? He pointed to himself

and then the bushes to his left. Then to me and the foliage to the right.

As if I'd hide. Instead, I hefted the stick I'd scrounged along our way and hollered, "Over here, assholes. Let's go."

Bane shook his head before heading into the scrub.

Me, I waited, and soon the rustling of branches let me know I had company. What I didn't expect? To be shot at.

I barely dodged the bullet that whistled by. "Well, that was unsporting," I yelled. And now that I knew they didn't want a clean fight, I could play dirty.

See, I didn't just have size and strength with an affinity for weapons. Part of what made me so good at my job? My ability to merge with shadows. Think of it as going invisible. I stepped into a dark spot and disappeared.

"Where'd she go?" someone shouted.

"Fuck her. We came for the Warden."

I glanced at the bushes he'd chosen to hide in and couldn't spot the man. Good job. Hopefully he'd stay put while I handled the threat.

Sticking to the gloomy pockets, I circled to the left and ended up behind the guy with the smoking gun. An arm around his neck choked off his air supply and ability to yell. He clawed at my arm and struggled. With a sharp twist, he died.

And now I had a gun. Ooh, and the knife sheathed at his side. Not a great knife. The edge of it was dull. Not ideal for slicing, but it would still do the clumsy job. His friends in the jungle could take it up with him in Hell when I killed them with it.

I tucked it in my waistband for now and took aim. Much like a certain Jedi knight in training, I didn't look with my eyes but my senses. Pivot. Shoot.

"Argh!"

Foliage rustled as more of the nine—now down to seven—came rushing in.

Bang.

Another bit the dirt.

Three down.

A scream to my right indicated the Warden most likely helped—or the jungle did.

A loud growl preceded the snapping and cracking of branches as my next foe came charging.

My shot to the heart didn't slow down the barrel-chested dude with a hairy face and tusks jutting from the side of his mouth and horns from his head. A quick aim put a bullet hole in his head.

The beast man teetered on his feet before collapsing, but before I could celebrate, another beast man behind him charged for me. Despite still standing in shadow, it was as if he could see me, or —judging by his flaring nostrils—smell.

And, of course, the piece-of-shit gun I'd taken from the guy who couldn't even keep his blade sharp jammed.

I tossed it at the beast and braced for impact. Or at least made it seem like I'd meet the charge. I sidestepped at the last moment and tripped the big fucker. He hit the ground face first, and before he could rise, I jumped on his back and began sawing at his neck with my dull blade.

Didn't get far before he grabbed and flung me. I flew! But my landing proved problematic, as it involved a tree. I hit hard enough I lost my grip on the knife.

The beast man loped for me, his neck too thick for me to easily snap, his hands big and most likely boulder-like if they connected. I had to weaken him somehow.

As he neared, I readied myself. The timing had to be just right. Kick.

I aimed for his kneecap, dislodging it with the force of my blow—which would have been more effective with my boots. Still, it caused the beast man to shriek in pain and rage. It also slowed him down as he limped, meaning I could dance around him.

My next attack took out his other knee, but from the back, causing him to buckle. He bellowed in rage as I darted in to kick him in the face while avoiding his flailing paws—because dude didn't have regular fingers, seeing as how they were hairy and clawed!

The noise he made as he grabbed his crushed nose made me miss the foe sneaking up on me. Only instinct had me ducking to the side and avoiding the swipe of another clawed monster man.

It wouldn't have been hard to avoid if the one at my back hadn't grabbed hold of my ankle. Fucker dragged me down and paid for it with a jab of my elbow to his neck. While he wheezed for air, I kicked the other attacker with strength that would have knocked a human on his ass.

The monster smiled and showed off a mouth full of jagged yellow teeth.

Before he could try chomping on me a la tartar, a massive leopard dropped from the tree and landed atop the monster. A huge jaw bit around the head, while claws dug in.

Since I wasn't needed for the kill, I concentrated on the man thinking he was stealthy as he crept for me with a gun pointed in my direction.

I stalked toward him, and he took aim. "Die, cunt!"

"As if I haven't heard that before," I grumbled

as I dodged the bullet he fired, moving fast, the adrenaline giving me the speed to rush the guy before he could pull the trigger again. I slammed into him hard enough air whooshed from him, and he hit the ground hard. An arm firmly pressed—and crushing—his neck made sure he no longer posed a threat.

Even better, his gun was mine. Not a real prize. "Poor baby." I crooned to the weapon, noting the rust and the mistreatment of what was once a beautiful Ruger. Some people just didn't know how to appreciate fine workmanship.

Turned out I didn't need it. There was nothing left to kill, unless the leopard counted. He eyed me calmly, sitting on his haunches, his green eyes reminding me of...

No way.

I squinted, before saying, "Bane, is that you?"

The reply? A grotesque shifting of body parts that turned a furry, four-legged feline into a naked hunk of a man.

My jaw dropped, not just because the Warden turned out to be a shape-shifting leopard. I eyeballed slabs of muscle, abs that made my knees weak, and a dick to put my toy at home to shame.

Whether he liked it or not, we would be hooking up. Which was why I smiled when I said, "I always wanted a cat."

9

The Warden

THE ASSASSIN SHOWED HIM NO RESPECT, and to make matters worse, she unabashedly ogled. Nudity didn't usually cause an issue. Shifters didn't keep their clothes when they morphed shapes, so having his dick out in front of folks wasn't new. What didn't usually happen? An erection. He turned away lest she see how eyeing him like a yummy piece of steak affected him.

His libido didn't care she was a crass killer. Then again, he shouldn't throw stones given the things he'd done.

As he hunted down his clothes, she rustled through the brush, speaking as if he listened—which he did.

"You miscounted, kitty. There were ten of the

enemy. Final kill count is six for me. Four for you. I win."

"Depends on how you count them. You took out several with bullets."

She snorted. "Nice try. A kill is a kill."

A good point. Another thing he'd noted? She'd not hesitated to act.

He emerged fully dressed to find Enyo on her knees inspecting one of the minotaurs.

"Do you often have people gunning for you?" she queried, tugging at a horn, which remained firmly attached.

"It happens from time to time."

She glanced at him over her shoulder. "Why?"

"Popular guy. I blame my warm personality."

At that, she snorted. "More like you have something they want. Why are they after you? What are you guarding? Is it that treasure room you mentioned?"

"Not quite."

"Gonna explain?"

"Not here and now. We should get moving in case there are more."

She rose, and he noticed she'd armed herself from the corpses with several knives and at least two guns. "How far to civilization?"

"Depends on if they sabotaged my helicopter."

She blinked. "You have a helicopter?"

"I told you I live on an island."

"Most people would use a boat."

"I have a few of those, too, and a private jet."

"A man with toys. You just get more and more interesting," she mused aloud.

His chest almost puffed with pride at her intrigue until he reminded himself to remain aloof. His self-imposed isolation must be getting to him. He didn't usually react so strongly to a woman. Blame the fact he'd not been intimate with anyone —unless his hand counted—in a few years.

"I see them more as necessary tools given my need for efficient transportation." He didn't like being at the mercy of other people's schedules.

"Which way is your ride?"

He pointed. "Northeast."

Without waiting for him, she set off, meaning he got to enjoy her rear view, well-toned and shapely. Her hips flared into muscled thighs. Her taut ass was heart-shaped without any jiggle. Her lustrous black hair, slopping out of its elastic, teased by the occasional breezes flitting through the branches. A tattoo hinted at the collar of her form-fitting tee, and he wondered how much ink the rest of her body sported. Not that he planned to find out.

No denying her appeal. He could see why some of those rich men let her get close. But she was a deadly kind of beauty, like the Venus flytrap that lured in its prey before snapping shut.

A good thing she'd only be around until the upcoming hybrid eclipse; otherwise, her claim they'd become lovers might come true. He knew better than to get entangled. For one, neither of them could afford to let down their guard, not this close to the event. The closer they got to the actual date, the more the attacks would mount.

As they walked, she didn't talk. At all. Nor did she make a sound. She prowled through the jungle, a true predator even if on two feet and not four. And he'd know. A shifter since birth, he'd been running in fur before he learned to walk. Hunting before his first birthday, according to his parents, who were now long dead.

She might not have his sense of smell, but she had an alertness about her, the way her head swiveled constantly, her eyes tracking. And she listened. Every sound drew her attention. Nothing escaped her notice. A trait that might just be sexier than her ass.

Fuck.

They emerged in the clearing to find his helicopter intact. Or so he hoped. While she scouted the inside for nasty surprises, he did a circle check on the rotors, looking for loose bolts or pieces. Essentially signs of sabotage.

Given the fact his foes wanted to capture and not kill him, he doubted any damage would happen in the air. The question being, would the chopper even fly? The only thing he couldn't verify was the fuel system. An additive would render his chopper a useless hunk of junk. Only one way to find out.

"Everything seems fine. Let's get going," he said, rounding the chopper to find her leaning against it, looking pale. "You okay?" She appeared nauseous, and they'd not even boarded the craft.

At his query, she straightened. "Fine. That rodent you fed me isn't sitting pretty."

"No puking in my helicopter," he admonished.

"I never puke," she grumbled as she clambered into the passenger seat.

He climbed into the pilot's side and put on his headset before handing her a pair. Once the engine started, she'd need them, not just to block the noise but if they wanted to talk.

She buckled in as he began flicking switches, bringing the rotors to life, the whine of the motor muted by his earpieces. When they lifted from the ground, he cast her a quick glance to see if she was nervous, but she appeared relaxed.

She caught him looking. "How long have you been flying?"

"Since I was a teen," he replied as they rose past

the tree line and the jungle spread out before them, puffy green clouds that hid everything below.

"A teen?" Surprise lilted her reply. "Who taught you?"

"My dad." The Warden before him. Not usually a role passed down in the family, but the blessing—a.k.a curse—was the one to choose when it needed a new host. He'd never been given a choice.

"I don't have a father."

"But I thought you said you had sisters. Different dad?"

"Given we're identical triplets, not likely.

The news had him blurting, "Did your mom have you via invitro with a sperm donor?" He expected a lashing. Instead, he got a chuckle.

"No, she had us the old-fashioned way. A one-night stand with a human that resulted in three babies at once."

"Did you ever try to look for him?" He found himself more curious than expected.

"Kind of hard without a name or even a picture. She won't even tell us where or how they met."

Once more his mouth ran away before his brain could stop it. "Sounds like she's hiding something."

"I'm sure she has her reasons." He felt more

than saw her gazing at him. "The leopard thing. How did that happen?"

"It wasn't from a bite in case you're wondering if it's contagious. Shifters are born, not made." He flew high above the jungle, watching for any glints of metal that might indicate someone planned to fire on them.

"Shifters in the plural. I take it you're not the only one."

"Hardly, although my type, leopard, is rare. Wolves tend to be the most common."

"I never realized they even existed. You're the first one I've ever met."

"Because we don't tend to advertise our existence. As you've probably learned by now, there are those who covet the abilities of others."

"And when they're not jealous, they're fearful. My mom goes on rants about the Inquisition and the Salem witch trials. She takes that kind of persecution rather personally."

Her mother wasn't wrong. "There will be shifters on the island, as well as other types of non-humans. It would be advisable to not make an issue of their visible differences."

"As long as they don't try to hurt me, we'll be fine. I like to think I judge people on merit, not appearance." A pause then she added, "Just so I'm forewarned, how different are we talking? More dudes with horns and fur?"

"No minotaurs. They tend to be rather simple-minded and prone to violence, hence why my enemies like them as henchmen."

"Ahem, I believe the proper term these days is henchpeople."

"Not in this case. There are no female mino-taurs, and they aren't the only nonhuman species to have sexist traits."

"If there's no bull women, how do they procreate?"

"Unpleasantly. Let's just say they aren't picky about their partners. Some of those couplings result in even more bestial traits. Those, like the ones we encountered today, would have been born of a human woman."

"Ew."

He didn't mention the part where the mothers didn't survive birth, as the monsters clawed their way out when ready. He changed the subject. "Given the transient nature of some of my guests, you can expect to encounter wizards, witches, shifters, and more. Their abilities will not be fla-grant. Then there are those who will be self-evi-dent. An ogre named Sam who lives in a cave on the beach. Gregory, a cyclops, who makes the best bread in town. There's Pietro and Pietra, twin gargoyles—"

"Gargoyles!" she exclaimed. "Holy shit."

"They are rather shy and only move about at night. There are some fairies, but they keep to themselves. Oh, and there's Melisandre, the mermaid who lives in the lagoon. And before you ask, no, mermen do not exist."

"Then how are mermaids created?"

He grimaced. "The aquatic version of bestiality."

"Fuck off. Seriously? Ew. Gross."

"Agreed, so can we change the topic?"

"With so many creatures of legend living on your island, how do you keep them secret?"

"Easy. First off, the island is only visible to non-inhabitants close to the eclipse. Secondly, no one is allowed to visit without vetting and invitation. Those who do learn about the island are sworn to secrecy."

"What if someone doesn't respect your privacy and blabs?"

"They die." Because he took the protection of the island and its inhabitants seriously. If he expected her to be shocked, he'd obviously already forgotten who he spoke with.

"I've had to eliminate a few people over the years

because they were a little too free with my family secrets," she admitted, and then she turned right back to business. "What kind of defenses does your island have to ensure no one visits without permission?"

"There is only a narrow route ships can take to get close enough to dock. The island is surrounded by jagged rocks that will tear out the hull of even the shallowest craft."

"Doesn't mean someone can't anchor offshore and swim in."

"Sharks make that scenario dangerous."

"But not impossible," she insisted.

"Melisandre is in contract with the marine life around the isle and provides warning of incursion."

"And if she doesn't? What if someone gets past her?"

"So many questions," he murmured.

"You said I'm the last line of defense in this mission, which you've yet to detail. I am assuming this island will be where you're expecting this showdown to happen."

"It is." He paused before continuing. "If the enemy were to get past Melisandre, then there would be Sam."

"Your beach ogre."

"Yes."

"And if they defeat him?"

"The townsfolk."

"Assuming they even know there's an enemy in their midst. What if your foes skip past the town and go straight for your home?"

"The gargoyles would provide warning."

"Unless they've been distracted. What about during the day? Aren't they asleep?"

He frowned as he glanced at her. "These defenses have served me well for over two decades."

Rather than reply to that, she had another question. "Then why do you need me? You said you have an army on standby. Don't tell me you give all your soldiers such an intense interview."

"Because you'll be more than a soldier. I need a personal bodyguard to watch over me during the eclipse when I am helpless." A thing he hated to admit. "During that vulnerable moment is when you'll be expected to provide the final line of defense should all else fail."

She patted his knee. "Don't worry, Spot. I'll keep you safe."

"Spot?"

"Well, Kitty is kind of overdone, don't you think? Spot suits you much better."

"How about using my name?"

"Spoilsport." She then pointed. "I see lights."

Indeed, the dark of the jungle suddenly gave way to pinpricks of illumination from the village spread across the shores of a beach.

"That's the last civilized place before the island, which is about an hour's flight with good winds. But before we head over, we'll have to refuel."

He aimed for the tallest building, three stories high with the top floor being reserved for his personal use. The rooftop held a landing pad that illuminated with bright lights at his approach, due to the beacon in his craft emitting a signal. The chopper landed with barely a bump, and he flicked switches, turning off the motor before removing his headset.

Before he could exit the chopper, Enyo had already disembarked and come around to his side. As he joined her, the hairs on his neck lifted, and he didn't need Enyo's soft, "There's someone waiting for us," to know they had company. Company hidden from sight.

A glance to the side showed the assassin had disappeared, the trick where she used shadows to cloak her presence, but her scent—and the strange attunement he had for her—let him track her steps as she circled to get behind whoever waited.

Not one to show fear, Bane strode forward, boldly snapping, "I know you're there. Show yourself."

"About time you showed up," stated John as he dropped his cloak of invisibility.

Bane relaxed at seeing his friend.

Enyo did her job and placed a knife against John's neck.

To his credit, John didn't panic and drawled, "Only you would emerge from the jungle with a sexy Amazonian goddess."

The jealousy that hit Bane fast and hard shocked. John had always been suave when it came to women. Why should he care if John turned his charm on Enyo?

Tell that to Bane's clenched fists.

His tension eased as Enyo shot him down with a tart, "Save it, Casanova. I prefer my men to have calloused hands."

Of which Bane owned two.

10

·)·)·)·◉·(·(·(·

As I put the intruder and his attempt at flirting in his place, Bane's face went through a strange range of emotions that ended in a smile when I mentioned calloused hands.

He should smile. I'd seen his fingers. Rough from work. The kind that would drag and cause friction over flesh.

Speaking of flesh, I still held a knife to his friend's throat. I stepped away but didn't apologize for doing my job as I stood to the side and observed.

Bane neared, saying, "I'm surprised to see you here. Weren't you studying those scrolls they found recently in that cave in Ireland?"

"Turned out to be nothing of interest, so I

thought I'd see how your latest interview went. Judging by the fact you didn't return alone, I assume you finally found a worthy candidate."

"She not only passed the trials with ease, she already countered an attack."

I didn't preen at his praise, but I came close.

"Impressive," declared his friend. With his blond hair and chiseled features, he could have modeled. He wore tan khakis and a button-up white shirt, open at the neck, the long sleeves rolled up. A sign he didn't live in the area full time, as the humid heat demanded less material.

"Not really. I've countered worse," I replied as I sauntered to my current employer. The fact I gave my back to Bane's associate was an indication I didn't consider him a threat.

"As you can see, she also doesn't lack for confidence," Bane dryly added. "Enyo, meet John Mosby, an old friend of mine."

"Given his soft hands, I'm going to say wizard." I'd wager my favorite blade he wasn't a warrior.

"I dabble in the arts, but my true passion is history. I'm actually a professor at the University of Saint Magnus."

"Never heard of it."

"It's not a big school, but they've got an incredible library in their catacombs."

"I'll have to tell my sister. She loves to read."

Maybe some old books in an old cave would be enough to drag Frieda out of her self-imposed isolation. Thinking of her had my stomach twinging. I turned to Bane. "Is there a phone I can use to call my siblings? They'll be worried about me."

"You can contact them once we reach the island. The lines there are secured."

Earlier he'd mentioned the island being an hour flight from here. Wherever "here" was. A glance around showed a town asleep. "Okay, but just so you know, I won't be responsible for whatever happens."

He frowned at me. "What's that supposed to mean?"

"My sisters can be overprotective."

"Of an assassin?" His tone emerged incredulous.

"Did you forget the part where I told you we're triplets?" I rolled my eyes because, duh, he should have remembered.

"There's three of you?" The surprise came from John, whom I'd almost forgotten about. I'm sure his ego would crush under the weight if he knew.

"Not exactly like me. I'm the tallest and meanest, although Dina might argue the mean part."

"Are they also assassins?" John queried, a man of questions.

"My sisters have their own specialties. Witch

and seer." No point in hiding it, especially since Bane and, by connection, this John, probably knew more about magic than we did. Mother never encouraged us going out looking for other users. "*You don't want to be used by the wrong sort.*"

In retrospect, I had to wonder at her motive in trying to shield us from what was proving to be a much bigger world than I'd expected. I mean a fucking leopard shapeshifter. How cool was that? Mom never let us have a pet growing up.

"Arcane triplets with power. Fascinating and unusual," John mused.

There was that word again. Arcane. I liked it better than paranormal and supernatural.

Bane cleared his throat. "Can we discuss this inside where there's whiskey and food?"

We headed for the door leading down into the penthouse suite that Bane said he rented out for his personal use. Given he lived on an island, it made sense to have a place on land to flit to and use as a jumping point for his leopard, because I'd wager, he liked running around in his fur.

John continued to ask questions. "Are your parents arcane-powered too?"

"Mom is a witch. But Dad was apparently human."

"Family name?"

"Grae. And before you ask, it's not spelled

Graeae like the legend about the three sisters. But we are named after them."

"I'm surprised I haven't heard of your family," John stated.

"Why would you? I've never heard of you," I pointed out.

"That would be because you've avoided being documented. Arcane families are part of my studies at the college. I track their lineages and their powers. Not only is it unusual for you to have survived to your obvious age without being noticed, but it's also unheard of in multiple births for all the children to show ability. Usually only one child inherits the power."

"Mom always did say we were special." She actually used to yell, *"You're a special brand of demons, I swear."* Not to defend her, but when we misbehaved, we did so in triplicate.

"Your sister the seer, is she any good at controlling her visions?" John just kept flapping his lips.

I shrugged. "Depends."

"What about the past? Can she see it as well?"

My lips pursed. "I don't know. You'd have to ask her." Given she'd never mentioned it to me, I was gonna say she probably either couldn't or never tried.

"I'd love to speak with her," John further stated. "I've been looking for a seer that can look into the past to help me with a book I've been trying to decipher."

Frieda would hate a stranger contacting her out of the blue. I smiled wide as I said, "I'll put you in touch." It would do her some good to have someone rattle her little bubble.

The penthouse we entered had all the elements of a tropical getaway. Wicker furniture. Floral drapes. A bar with bottles. But I was more interested in the bowl of fruit. I'd expended a lot of energy in the fight and subsequent walk. My body needed refueling.

As I ate, Bane told his friend of the minotaurs and armed men we'd encountered.

Which led to John replying, "I took care of a group in town trying to rent a boat."

"Where did you leave their bodies?" Bane asked casually.

I almost choked on the banana I ate.

"Dumped in the next bay for the sharks. But we both know they were just the beginning. I expect the town will get overrun with those looking for you as the time gets closer. It's already much more active compared to the last time."

Interesting. So John truly had been around a while. I kept listening.

"I'm aware. And you know preparations have

been made. Enyo was the last piece." A nod in my direction.

Listening to them, I had to point out the obvious. "If you didn't want them to find you, maybe renting a whole hotel floor to store your helicopter isn't the best idea."

He grimaced. "I'll admit we got comfortable. Since the last time was a cakewalk, I didn't expect things to escalate like they have. And I don't know if hiding would help. The island acts as a magnet. The closer we get to the hybrid eclipse, the stronger the draw."

"Why not incapacitate the boats to ensure no one can rent them?" I provided what seemed like a simple solution.

"For one, it would deprive some people of their livelihoods and food. Second, they'd just rent or steal some from the next town."

A reply to which John coughed before saying, "I, um, might have placed a temporary spell on all the ships currently docked that won't let them steer anywhere but east or west, meaning they can't be used to get to the island. It should wear off sometime after the eclipse."

I clapped. "That's actually brilliant. Good to see your friend is thinking since you aren't."

Bane scowled. "I don't want to see people getting hurt because of frustrated assholes."

"If that happens, just let me know. I'm always happy to punish them," I volunteered.

Bane sighed. "Why don't you grab a shower while I work on getting the chopper refueled?"

"You might want to hold off on flying until morning. Weather report has a small squall heading our way," John informed.

Judging by Bane's grimace, he didn't want to wait, but rather than be ornery and insistent about keeping to his schedule, he nodded. "We'll leave in the morning." Bane glanced my way. "There's three guest bedrooms to choose from." He waved a hand at the doors.

"Where are you sleeping?" I asked. "I'll set up a defensive position in that room."

He crossed his arms. "I don't need you hovering vulture-like over me while I sleep."

"Don't whine. You're the one who hired me to do a job, and I can't do it if I'm in another room."

"If someone attacks, you'll hear. The walls aren't thick," Bane argued.

"Unless you're dead. Or knocked out."

"She has a point," John interjected.

Bane glared at his friend. "You're not helping."

I smirked before adding a teasing, "What's wrong? Afraid I'll kill you in your sleep?"

I expected an angry retort, but instead, I got a

drawled, "More like defending your delicate feminine sensibilities since I sleep naked."

"So do I," I sauced back as I sauntered for the double doors that could only be the master. I entered into a luxurious haven with a massive bed, sliding doors leading to a balcony, and an ensuite with a glassed-in shower. I checked all the spaces someone could hide: under the bed, closet, the balcony outside. I re-entered to find a pile of clothes on the bed. It would be nice to get out of my stinking gear.

I bathed quickly, getting the jungle off me and then combing my hair into a wet plait with the brush I found wrapped in plastic. Walking out in a towel, I went hunting in his closet for clothes since the garments that had been left on the bed proved more girly than I liked, not to mention too small for a woman of my size. The top cropped at midriff on my long torso. The skirt way too flowery.

Raiding Bane's closet netted me a polo shirt of solid blue and white khakis, which I belted tight. For shoes I had the choice of flip-flops, my grungy sneakers, or nothing. I went with nothing for the moment. Back in the main living area, I found my new employer sitting by a table quietly talking with his friend, a platter of food set before them.

His gaze went up and down, but he said

nothing at my appropriation of his clothes. If he had, I would have stripped and tossed them at him.

As I sat, I asked, "So, what did you plot while I was showering?"

"We were discussing you," Bane declared.

"Me?" I ignored the flutter because he didn't mean it in a boy-likes-girl way but as an employer checking up on his investment.

"I was telling John that Lance recommended you."

"Lance being?"

"A good friend. Also a magic user, but of a different sort from John. He's more into infusing objects. He's the one who made the teleport ball that brought you. He's been dabbling in attack magic as well."

"And you trust him?"

"Why wouldn't I?"

I shrugged. "You're a dude in charge of a big secret. You can't be dumb enough to not realize some folks might want to use you."

He frowned. "I have no reason to suspect anyone close to me."

Maybe he didn't, but part of my job was to trust no one. "Are all your friends wizards?" I asked, biting into a bun that had been warmed and was crunchy on the outside.

"No."

"How did this Lance hear about me?" I picked at some cheese and cold cuts.

"Said you did a job for his mother years ago. In Paris. A local mobster wouldn't leave his sister alone, and so his mother hired you to handle it."

It took me only a second to place the mission. "Ah yes, Jean Louis the stalker. He blubbered like a baby before I tossed him off a balcony."

John appeared discomfited, but Bane nodded. "Lance says his mother was quite happy about how quickly you handled matters."

Quickly because I couldn't be gone for long from my sisters. "I don't like to fuck around. Once I get a job, I get it done. I'm surprised your friend didn't handle it himself."

"Lance's mother didn't want him implicated," Bane's reply.

"Not after the last incident, where he was less than discreet," John's quiet murmur.

"Meaning what?"

Bane grimaced. "I don't know the details other than he lost his temper and someone got hurt. It cost his family a pretty penny to cover up."

I might have remarked about the company he kept, but given I shoved someone in front of a subway for smacking into my sister and spilling her hot coffee on her white blouse, I couldn't really cast any stones.

John glanced at Bane. "Speaking of cover-up, have you warned her about the danger?"

I rolled my eyes. "Hello, sitting right here. And I think I got an idea of the danger with that attack in the jungle, which I handled. Without any of my usual weapons, I might add." I glanced at Bane. "I am going to need to arm myself."

"I have an arsenal at the castle—"

"Hold on, castle?" This kept getting better and better.

"Yes. And within, there are guns, knives, swords, even crossbows."

"Ready to wage war?"

He shrugged. "The Warden is supposed to be prepared to repel enemy forces at all times."

"Yet you don't have a standing army."

"In the off years, we only keep a minimal number of guards. Given the monster activity, I've had to hire some mercenaries from an arcane guild. Not cheap," he grumbled.

Given his age, he would have lived through at least one of these events, if not more. Hybrid eclipses, while extremely rare, did occur every ten years or so.

Before I could ask him about it, John yawned. "It's well past my bedtime. I assume we'll be heading to the island early."

"You're coming with us?" I asked then added,

"Hope you're okay sitting in my lap on the chopper."

That raised his brows in surprise, but Bane chuckled. "We'll take the yacht over."

"You really know how to make a job look good. First a tropical waterfall, then a helicopter ride, and now a cruise. This is turning out to be the best vacation. You couldn't have painted a bigger target. I am going to get so much exercise," I teased.

"This isn't a joke," Bane growled.

"Who's laughing? I am totally psyched for this. Now say goodnight to your friend and off to bed," I chirped while John gaped.

"I am really second-guessing my test results," Bane complained.

"If you ask me, you could have been tougher. Now, get your butt moving. Can't have the boss too tired."

To John's barely concealed mirth, Bane trudged to his bedroom with me following.

While he hit the bathroom, I parked a chair by the sliding door, off to the side, hidden by a potted plant and drapes. When he emerged, he noticed me in my spot and frowned.

"You won't be comfortable sleeping there."

"I've slept in worse."

"I need you well rested."

"You're paying me to be ready if we're attacked."

"I'm sure you'll be just as quick getting out of bed as a chair," he argued.

"Why, Bane, is this your way of saying you'd like to cuddle? I should warn you I like to be the big spoon."

He rolled his eyes heavenward and groaned. "Why me?"

"Because you wanted the best and you got it."

He fixed me with a stare. "I'm not going to fuck you. I don't give a damn what your sister said."

My lips tilted. "Tell you what, I won't make the first move. I will leave it all up to you, Spot."

"Good. Because it will never happen."

"If you say so," I sang.

"I know so," he insisted. "Now, I'm going to bed. Sleep in the chair or the bed. I don't care. See you in the morning." With that, he turned out the light and stripped.

He really did sleep naked, and I saw enough of that body in the streaming light of the three-quarter moon to wish I'd not vowed to leave the seduction up to him.

I sat in the chair and dozed, thinking about my sisters, knowing they had to be worried. I'd call them in the morning and break the news they'd have to meet me in paradise. Because no way would

I be able to defend Bane if I was dealing with the separation sickness that plagued us when apart.

I had no clue where in the world I'd ended up, but I'd figure it out so my sisters could join me. Ooh, maybe we could get his wizard friend to send us some teleportation balls. Ha. Wouldn't Dina shit a brick. Actually, Frieda would shit two because she'd have to leave the house.

I'd have to make sure she loved it. Set them up in a luxurious suite or villa on the beach, hire a handsome pool guy or two to keep the occupied while I dealt with my mission.

I dozed on and off and had the strangest dream.

11

Bane

·⊃·⟩·⟩·⊙·⟨·⟨·⟨·

THE DREAM BEGAN AS IT ALWAYS DID, WITH a knock at the door of his uncle's cottage. His parents had sent him to stay there. "To keep you safe," his mother claimed, kissing him on the cheek and hugging him goodbye before they set off on the long drive back to the island.

"We'll see you in a few days," his father added. In a few days, the hybrid eclipse would be over, and their home would be safe for a young man once again.

He'd been left in the care of Uncle Rupert. Brother to his father, an ornery man who'd agreed to mind his nephew during the last few days before all hell broke loose.

This would be the second hybrid eclipse he'd

lived through, but the first he'd actually remember and understand.

Understood he was being shunted aside because his parents feared he'd be a liability.

"We don't want anything to happen to you." His mother's claim.

"I can help," Bane argued. "You've seen my training."

"You're still too young," Mother replied.

His father put a hand on his shoulder. "It will be fine. We've been through this before." A blasé addition.

All Bane heard? *We don't need you.*

It didn't help his abrupt uncle grumbled about having him underfoot. Never mind the fact Bane stayed clear of him, spending most of his time in the field behind his uncle's house, exercising to burn off his irritation at being sequestered. No cell service or cable in this remote place meant no contact with his parents or his friends.

"'It's safer if no one knows where you are.'" Because despite there never being any issues in the past, suddenly his parents feared their enemies would try to use him. As if he'd aid their foes. He understood the important role his father played. A guardian against an ancient evil. One that could never be released from its prison.

An important task that his father inherited after

the last Warden died of old age, which his mother used as evidence that all would be fine. "'Joseph lived to eighty-four and died in his bed. Your father will too.'"

"Then why are you sending me away?"

"It's just a precaution," Mother stated, brushing the hair from his forehead. She'd always done that to soothe him as far back as he could remember. And soon she'd do it for the child she carried. A sibling that had caused much surprise to his parents in their forties, not that her stomach showed any signs of it yet, given it was early.

He'd tried to use it as an argument to stay. "You should be resting."

"I'm pregnant, not an invalid," was her dry reply. She'd gone on to prove her claim by continuing with her rigorous training routine. See, Father was The Warden, tasked with keeping the key safe and the prison locked, and Mother? She acted as his bodyguard. It was how they'd fallen in love. When his father became anointed as the new Warden, he held an open competition the year before the hybrid eclipse, and she won, to the surprise of all. Not because of her sex, but the fact a human beat out shifter and magic-user alike with her cleverness.

A second knock came while Bane moped in the tiny attic room he'd been staying in. Uncle had been quite firm on the fact he shouldn't answer the door, to conceal his presence. Even when he trained outside, he kept his features hidden with a toque, big sunglasses, and bulky sweater. If anyone asked, he was to lie about his true name. As if he'd run into anyone. The rutted lane to his uncle's cottage didn't play nice with cars.

A glance out the window showed no vehicle parked, not even a bike. Odd, especially given the next closest home was a few miles away. It seemed strange someone would have walked over. Perhaps a driver had broken down on the road and seen the path. They'd be in for a rude surprise when Uncle sent them on their way. His idea of charity barely extended to minding Bane for a few days.

He'd overheard his parents discussing it on the way over when they thought him asleep.

"You know Rupert's never forgiven me for becoming The Warden," his father had softly murmured.

"It's not like you did it on purpose." The previous Warden had several apprentices by the time of his death, Rupert being one of them. Only the Warden's Key, the thing that passed from one to the next, had a mind of its own. It skipped those vying for the position and settled on a brother visiting at the time. Apparently, this wouldn't be the first time the key proved contrary.

Downstairs, a third knock finally had his uncle

answering. Bane couldn't hear who came calling, only the reply.

"Don't know who you're talking about. Git." He heard his uncle's voice rise with annoyance as whoever visited made a demand he didn't like.

Bane crept to his door and opened it a crack to listen.

"Give us the boy and you won't come to harm."

"Fuck right off or the one getting hurt will be you." No mistaking the sound of the shotgun being cocked. Uncle kept one by the door for scaring the foxes that liked to hunt his hens.

"So be it."

What happened next proved unclear, other than it involved some thumping and a cry of pain.

Uncle Rupert!

Forgetting the warnings, Bane fled down the steps from the peaked second floor to find his uncle on the floor, his temple bleeding, his eyes shut. The rise of his chest showed him unconscious, not dead.

The cause? The stranger standing in the doorway. The not-very-tall dude wore a jacket too large that hung on his thin frame. Pale features stretched taut over sharp cheeks and accented eyes glowing orange.

A wizard. Here. Bane didn't need the sudden knot in his stomach to know who he'd come for.

The stranger's gaze shifted from Rupert to

Bane. "There you are. Son of the Warden." The wizard offered a smile that twisted Bane's guts.

"Get out." Bane moved to stand by his uncle, fists clenched, ready to fight. His body bristled as his leopard snarled, wanting to show this jerk what he thought of his actions.

"I'll leave, but you're coming with me." The man beckoned with his hand, and Bane felt a strange tug, as if he were a metal being drawn to a magnet.

Gritting his teeth, he fought the sensation.

The stranger's brows lifted. "I see we're going to do this the hard way."

"Leave the boy alone!" Uncle Rupert shouted, suddenly recovered enough to fire his gun.

Only the buckshot never connected. It hit an invisible wall and halted midair.

The stranger's lips parted in a grotesque smirk. "I gave you a chance." He flicked his hand, and the pellets went flying back in the direction they'd been fired, hitting his uncle, who cried out as he once more hit the floor, only this time he bled. Uncle's body rippled as his animal tried to emerge, only to fail. Blame the buckshot threaded with silver.

The same restriction didn't constrain Bane. His scream of rage turned into a snarl as the shift came upon him, his mighty feline bursting from clothes and skin. He leapt, only to find himself caught in a vise of magic, held aloft over the floor.

"Like father, like son, I see." The man shook his head.

Bane snarled and writhed, feeling the magic netting him in its grip, fighting against it hard enough he broke free!

It surprised the wizard, and that distraction allowed Bane to swipe, his claws raking across the man's face. The stranger reeled and stumbled out the door. Bane followed, but before he could do more damage, he was picked up and thrown back into the house. He hit the kitchen table and skidded across it, his agile feline grace failing him as he landed awkwardly on the other side. He rose and shook his head as the stranger came for him, his face bleeding from the deep scratches, flanked by a monster. Or so it seemed, given the horns curling from its forehead and its reddish, almost leathery skin.

A demon. A thing he'd learned about, but his father had claimed were beyond rare.

The stranger pointed at him. "Get me the boy."

The demon stalked for Bane, a massive, towering threat that he didn't want to fear but did. Could his claws shred its thick skin? Would it even bleed?

"Unholy beast! I banish thee." The unlikely cry came from his uncle, rising despite his many wounds, holding out a cross that shone bright. Bright enough the demon screamed.

Uncle Rupert advanced on the demon, who fled from the magical artifact, bellowing as it ran out of the cottage past the bleeding stranger.

Together, Bane and his uncle faced the man who'd dared attack them. A man who no longer looked so cocky without his demon guard.

Bane took a step and snarled.

The stranger dug a hand into his pocket and withdrew an orb, which he clutched tight. As it shrank, it enveloped him in a light and he disappeared from sight. But the trauma he'd caused remained.

The danger gone, Bane shifted to his human shape and rushed to his bleeding uncle. "We need to clean your wounds."

"No time for that. We need to leave. Get dressed," his uncle snapped.

Bane fled to his room and grabbed clothes, putting them on quickly before heading back downstairs to see his uncle at the sink, trying to rinse off some of the blood.

His uncle sagged, and Bane caught him. "You need a doctor."

"Bah. It's mostly flesh wounds. What we need is to get out of here before that prick comes back with more of his minions."

"Who was he?"

"An asshole who thinks to use you against your father. Let's go. Grab my keys. You'll have to drive," his uncle stated. The request only reinforced the seriousness of his injuries.

They emerged into the night, the stars and moon covered by thick clouds. Bane took the driver's seat, while his uncle slumped in the passenger side.

He put the car in Drive and carefully began moving, only to have his uncle bark, "Can you not find the fucking gas pedal?"

He increased the speed but winced at the beating the car took. The headlights were weak twin beams that did little to illuminate the dark rutted path.

His uncle's wheezing breaths didn't help Bane's anxiety as they bounced along the bumpy track. His sweaty hands clutched the wheel.

"Where are we going?" he asked. The nearest town with a doctor was a good forty minutes away.

"As far from here as we can."

"We should call my parents and tell them what's happened." When his uncle didn't reply, a glance to the side showed him slumped, eyes closed, breathing shallowly.

Shit. Shit. Shit.

He faced forward in time to see a massive figure stepping into the road in front of him. The demon.

No time to brake, and honestly, he didn't give a shit about the monster. He aimed straight for it.

Thump.

The body of the monster hit the grill and flopped onto the hood, smashing through the windshield, the massive face snarling in his direction, teeth clacking.

"Argh!" Bane kept his foot on the gas, despite being unable to see. The car smashed into a tree, and the airbags deployed.

It took him a moment to shake off the daze from the impact. A moment to realize he could only hear his ragged, agitated breath and the ticking of the cooling engine. By the time he fought free of the airbag, he panted hard, panicked as he realized he smelled blood. Too much blood. Thankfully, it came from the demon, whose eyes had clouded over with death.

"Uncle Rupert?" He called his uncle's name as he pummeled at the airbag on the passenger side, his fear heightening as he realized he couldn't hear any sign of life. The sightless eyes of his uncle brought a wail. "No."

Tears brought no solution to his dilemma though. Alone. Bruised. His uncle dead. A demon slumped on the hood. A wizard gunning for him.

What to do?

Sticking around would only get him caught up in a legal nightmare. A few calming breaths and he remembered his lessons. The primary one being: Never get caught.

"I'm sorry, Uncle. Rest in peace." Whispered as he dragged his uncle into the driver's seat. Then using a lighter—for the cigarettes he wasn't supposed to smoke—he tore a strip of fabric from his uncle's jacket, trying to hold back the tears that threatened. He put one end in through the gas cap, feeding it until only the tip showed, and then he lit it and walked away.

Hands jammed in his pockets, his pace rapid, his eyes wet, he'd walked a fair distance when the car blew and then burned. It would be a while before anyone found the wreck, hopefully long enough for the fire to remove all evidence.

It took him a full two days of walking and hitchhiking before he made it to the small shore town his parents visited when they needed to get away from the island. An island that moved. Currently stationed and hidden off the coast of Ireland, it shifted locations depending on where the next hybrid eclipse would occur. Hidden from human methods of observation, and usually from the arcane too, until the alignment of the moon and sun.

It wasn't hard to steal a boat to bring him over,

all the while watching the sky. The eclipse was almost upon them, and he couldn't help but feel a sense of urgency. It drove him to run the engine hotter and faster than he usually dared.

When the island came in sight, he didn't slow down. Mostly because he realized the magical cloak that hid the island had completely failed. It began glitching in the weeks leading up to the eclipse. A normal thing, his father claimed.

Bane threaded between the rocks to the quay. A quay covered in blood and bodies. Not all of them human. He saw mostly monsters. Or at least things that didn't talk.

Creatures from the sea, sporting pinchers, but also a few goblins. Probably rowed over on the flotsam rafts bumping the sea wall by the quay.

Dead along with them were soldiers clad in combat gear, weapons still gripped in some cases. Judging by their green pallor, poisoned. They wore arcane badges, a purple squiggle that identified them as working for the arcane guild of fighters. The AGOF.

It appeared his parents had lied. They'd hired an army.

Dread filled his stomach as he quickly tied off his boat and ran toward the castle he called home. More bodies lined the road. People he didn't recognize in combat gear, but a few he did know, like Greta, the sweet, rotund matron who baked the best pies, and Langley, an avian shifter who'd come here after losing his mate. Then there were more of the monsters, a name to sum them all up. Another demon like the one he'd encountered, minotaur, even orcs.

So much death. The moon and the sun marched relentlessly closer, rousing his fear. Please don't let him be too late. He regretted that five-minute stop for food. He raced for the castle.

He came across no one living.

Not one person.

The island didn't have many inhabitants, but they did have a good twenty or so. Did they hide, or did they lie amongst the corpses?

Entering his home, he stopped abruptly at the sight of blood smearing the flagstone floor and streaking a wall. A table that usually held flowers, broken by the body slumped atop it. An undine, a grotesque creature with wrinkled and slimy skin over a lumpy frame.

Bane made only a single detour before heading for the entrance to what his mom called the dungeon. He needed a weapon. He couldn't count on his feline once he went below. Magic failed in the chamber with the portal. Something in that area prevented it, and that included shifting. Holding out his blunt fingers and snarling with human lips wouldn't scare anyone.

The training room remained untouched. A dichotomy given the usual place of violence was the only one without actual blood. He grabbed his sword and dagger, wishing he dared take the time to grab a gun from the vault, but urgency demanded he move.

Faster.

He pounded down the steps to the dungeon, seeing more signs of violence. People he knew, too. Some of them dead, others groaning as they put pressure on their wounds. At least some might survive.

As he neared the next door, he spotted Killian, who'd dangled him on his knee. The big man sat slumped, holding a wound in his side. He noticed Bane and grunted. "You're not supposed to be here."

"Where are my parents?"

Killian's gaze flicked to the portcullis that was usually shut before saying, "Leave now while you can."

Abandon his parents? Never.

He rushed past, his feet pounding the stone steps that circled round and round as he descended into the bowels of the castle. The sounds and cries of a battle wafted, and for a moment he debated doing as Killian said and running.

But he wasn't a coward.

Bane burst out of the stairwell into a massive cavern, a place he'd never been allowed to visit because his father refused to show him. "Bad enough I got stuck with the curse. I won't have it take you, too, son."

He had no time to admire the grandeur of this mysterious chamber hidden under the castle. His gaze slid over the mosaics carved into the rock. He had eyes only for his parents across a sea of fighting bodies.

His father stood out with his hands glowing a light mauve against a column of pure white stone.

As if he sensed Bane's arrival, Dad's head turned to show eyes wide open, his anxiety plain to see.

Mom stood guard, gun in one hand, blade in the other. Her hair wisped messily around her bloodied face. She fired at the demons that encroached until she had no more bullets.

Four demons against his mom.

With a battle cry that gave Bane shivers, she went at them with her sword, fluid and savage. She sliced her way through the first wave of attack.

But more took their place at the goading of the stranger who'd come for Bane at Uncle Rupert's home. The wizard, his face healed but red with thick ugly scars. The fucker screamed at the demons to attack. They obeyed, and his mother danced amongst them.

Bane ran for her, determined to help, ignoring how the room darkened in warning. A humming vibrated his ears painfully. The darkness deepened, broken only by the pillar which glowed white. Magic slammed down, flattening those in the room, but not those on the dais.

His mother grimaced but remained standing, sword tip down, hunched over it. Dad still had his hands on the glowing pillar, the surface of which rippled and the air shimmered.

A demon pushed himself up from the floor behind Mom. She didn't see him, and when Bane tried to shout, no sound emerged. Father also saw, and his head dipped.

Why didn't he act? He had a dagger by his side.

Bane fought the magical hand pushing him down. Gritted against it, determined to reach the dais, even managed a few steps closer until the force proved too strong. He fell to his knees. Could only watch in horror as the demon snuck up and sliced her sword arm, leaving it limp.

And Father still didn't help her. He kept his hands pressed to the seam of the doorway, holding it shut, and while the Warden held it shut to keep evil from escaping, his mother fell to her knees before the demon that lifted its hand.

Save her. He screamed, to no avail. He remained voiceless, and too far away.

Father chose duty, and thus Mother died while he watched. Bane wailed, emitting a grief so sharp it cut through the magic holding him down. He raced for the dais, even as he knew he was too late for his mom. But maybe he could save his dad.

The pale stranger stood behind his father with a knife that gleamed. And still Father did not remove his hands. Didn't act. Didn't defend.

Bane ran as hard as he could but couldn't make it in time.

The knife struck.

Dad slumped.

Only seconds after, Bane slammed into the bastard who'd killed his family, the dagger he'd managed to hold on to digging deep before he wrenched it, ending the wizard's miserable life.

Too late.

As he shoved the corpse aside, he saw his father in a pool of blood, hands still pressed to that miserable column as the eclipse passed, leaving him an orphan, alone—

The nightmare abruptly ended as water poured over his face.

Startled awake, Bane blinked wet lashes, disoriented, especially given the sight of the two women standing at the foot of his bed.

One of them held a dagger that glowed, and in a dulcet voice, she said, "My name is Deino Grae. You stole my sister. Prepare to die!"

12

⁓⁙⁙⁙⁙⁙⁙⁓

AFTER A NIGHT OF SLEEPING ONLY IN spurts, plagued by a repeated strange dream, I hit the bathroom to handle some business. Like, literally, only a few minutes, and yet I emerged to find my sisters here—not entirely unexpected—and threatening Bane.

And what did he do?

Laughed. "Did you just parody *The Princess Bride*?"

Given Dina watched that movie a hundred times when we were young, most likely.

"Where is she? Tell me now before I shank you." Dina shook her dagger at him.

He didn't look the least bit concerned. He lay in bed, arm tucked under his pillow and head, the sheet revealing the upper part of his naked chest. Exactly why had I chosen to sleep in a chair instead of spooning his big body?

While Dina attempted to look menacing, Frieda glanced over and saw me. Her eyes widened, and I held a finger to my lips. Excuse me for getting my entertainment for the day.

"Shank me?" Bane couldn't contain his humor. "This isn't a prison. And your sister isn't my captive. I hired her to do a job."

"Hiring involves an interview process, not kidnapping her with magic!" Dina shrieked.

"What's going on?" John, his blond hair standing in tufts, came stumbling into the room, only to halt at the incongruous sight.

Before anyone got hurt, I cleared my throat. "Stand down, everyone."

Dina whirled. "You're alive."

I rolled my eyes. "Duh. Like you didn't already know." I felt her through our bond. She felt me. This was all for show.

"You contacted them? I told you the phones here weren't secure," Bane grumbled.

"She didn't call. Why do you think we jumped a red-eye flight to get here?" Dina whirled back to point her dagger again. "We were worried! She never leaves without warning."

"How did you know where to find her?"

He glanced at me and frowned. "Do you have some kind of tracking device implanted inside you?"

"Not exactly. Think of it as sisterly intuition. We always know where we all are at all times," I explained.

"And you didn't think to mention this?"

I shrugged. "I told you I had to call them."

"You could have told me they'd be hysterical."

My lips curved. "And miss all the fun? If it helps, I thought they'd at least wait twenty-four hours, especially since Frieda knew I'd be meeting with you."

Poor Frieda wrung her hands. She must not have seen any of this coming. Good. Let her see what it felt like for everyone else. It did her good to be caught by surprise once in a while.

Her lips turned down as she stated, "I told you to turn the Warden down, but as usual, you don't listen."

"What can I say? You were right. He made me an offer I couldn't refuse." For some reason my claim had both my sisters eyeing his half-naked upper body. I didn't like it one bit.

"I can just imagine," Dina murmured.

"We aren't sleeping together," I retorted.

"Sure you aren't," Dina scoffed. "Let me guess. You didn't have enough bedrooms in this place and his clothes magically fell off him when you went to bed."

"I slept in the chair." I pointed to it. Although I'd been tempted more than once to join him in bed. Especially since every time I closed my eyes, I fell into a strange dream that ended in some woman dying while a man did nothing, holding on to a pillar.

A man who looked like an older version of Bane.

"Anyone care to explain to me what's going on?" Poor John looked quite confused.

"These are my sisters, Frieda and Dina." I indicated each in turn then inclined my head at the half-naked—and flaunting it—Bane. "That's my new boss, the Warden, and his friend, John Mosby, a professor."

"Nice to meet you." John actually offered a sort of bow that had Frieda blushing for some reason. Could it be because John appeared to only be wearing bottoms? If he weren't so blond, I might have been more interested, but I preferred my men big and darker.

Like Bane.

Since the man in question appeared ready to fling off the covers and dazzle my sisters with his manhood, I clapped my hands. "Everyone out. Dina, you wrangle us some breakfast. Frieda, check the weather forecast and local events with your ability. We leave within the—" I glanced at Bane.

"Hour?" he questioned with an arched brow.

I nodded. "Hour."

Everyone left, and the door closed. Before I could say a word, he did. "I get the impression your sisters will be joining us."

"We kind of don't have a choice. Think of it as a triplet curse. We can't stay apart for long without getting sick, so where one goes, we all go."

"And you didn't think to mention it?"

"Perhaps next time, before you ambush someone for a job, you should try interviewing them first."

"How bad is the separation issue? How far and how long can you be away from them?"

"The right question is, what can they do to help?"

"It will be dangerous."

"No shit. But don't worry. My sisters can handle themselves." Well, Dina could at any rate. Frieda tended to be the warning system.

The covers flung back, and I got an eyeful of man. So much naked flesh. I stared. I knew I shouldn't, but damn.

He noticed, and the damn got a lot bigger.

He growled. "Stop eyeing me like I'm a juicy steak."

"If you didn't want me looking, you'd have asked me to leave before flaunting."

"Would you have gone?"

"No." My lips curved. "But if you insist on maintaining your modesty, I will turn my back."

"Look all you want. But don't touch," he warned as he stalked to the bathroom, revealing a taut ass that would have looked better with teeth marks.

"Wait, does that ban on touching include myself? Because we might have to discuss that since masturbation is a great stress reliever."

He made an inarticulate sound as he slammed the bathroom door.

I grinned. Just because I promised I wouldn't be the one to make the first move didn't mean I wouldn't tease.

A wander to the balcony showed the sun just cresting over the horizon. Absolutely beautiful if I ignored the blood on the beach and the bodies being dragged off.

Bane joined me and murmured, "I see we almost had visitors last night."

"I've heard of chick magnet, but you're the first monster one I've met." Kind of exciting. I couldn't wait to pit my skills against new foes. Those minotaurs had whetted my appetite.

"And this is the worst they've ever been. Even my father never saw them this bad."

"Think they have a clue as to why they're drawn?" I turned to eye him. He'd remained only partly naked. Shorts covered his lower half. Pity. He might have convinced me morning sausage could be better than bacon.

"No, but it's not just me they go after. The island has been targeted as well."

"Your own fault for advertising your presence."

"We'll do better in the next place."

I blinked, but his words still didn't make sense. "What do you mean the next place? Does the portal move?"

"In a sense. The day after the eclipse, between one breath and the next, without even a jolt, we'll find ourselves in a completely different place."

"It teleports you?"

"Not just me. The whole island. Part of its defense. It will spend days, sometimes months or years, in one spot before shifting locales, depending on circumstances."

"Circumstances being?"

"The main trigger is being noticed. If too many loose-lipped people know of its location, the island somehow finds out, and poof." He exploded his hands. "We suddenly find ourselves in a new spot.

The island also moves the year before the eclipse to a place with maximum exposure."

"What if it's on land?"

"Hasn't happened in my lifetime, but I did find a reference to a flood and a Warden named Noah."

I squinted suspiciously at him. "Now I know you're fucking with me."

He shrugged. "I've yet to verify the authenticity of that reference or another that seems to think my island is the fabled Atlantis."

"It would seem to me that the fact the island moves to an ideal coordinate is a bit of a flaw, as it allows the enemy to gather and plot their way onto the island."

"Not usually possible in the normal years, as the island's magic protects it from being found. Only those who have the Warden's permission to visit can come and go. Everyone else just passes on by. However, that cloaking and protective feature fades as the eclipse nears."

"That's some seriously intense magic shit."

"I'm aware."

Since he seemed talkative and I wasn't ready for my sisters yet, I mentioned my dream because only idiots ignored them, especially in my family. "You wouldn't know anything about a white pillar that glows, would you?"

He stiffened. "Why are you asking?"

"Last night, I dreamt about a chamber I've never seen before. It was massive, the stone carved and domed with a hole in the roof letting in daylight. The room was full of people fighting. Monsters and humans. They all seemed to be trying to get to this platform with a white column on it."

"You dreamt this?"

I nodded then added, "Some guy had his hands pressed to it while some chick fought a red-skinned demon. She ended up falling, and a skinny dude waiting in the wings stabbed the guy touching the glowing pillar."

The ice in his eyes could have frozen the ocean. "Those were my parents."

I blinked. "Wait, what?"

"It would appear you shared part of my nightmare."

It took me only a second to say the wrong thing. "You watched your parents die." Too late did I realize it sounded like an accusation when I'd meant it for a "hey, that sucks" kind of comment.

His face twisted. "Not by choice. They'd sent me away, but I was attacked. I tried to return to help but arrived too late. Once the eclipse struck, I couldn't move to save them."

"Why didn't your dad do something?" It struck me how he'd not budged once.

"Because he was keeping the portal closed. That

is the function of the Warden during the hybrid eclipse." A stiff reply.

"Portal to where?"

Again, his shoulders rolled. "I don't know."

"But you're the Warden."

"Not by choice. My father died upholding his duty, and upon his death, the burden landed on me."

"Damn."

"Indeed. Especially since it didn't come with much instruction. My father taught me what he knew, but even he never understood what we guarded against."

"Must be something nasty considering the demons and stuff trying to set it free." My expression turned thoughtful. "Does that kind of intense attack happen on each hybrid eclipse?"

He shook his head. "My father's predecessor only ever had to deal with strays that would show up. Usually only a dozen or so, and none ever reached the portal."

"You think this time will be different?"

"Yes." His jaw tensed. "My former bodyguard was killed a few months ago eating some bad soup. At the time, I thought it might be an accident, but since then, we've had issues."

"Such as?"

"Contaminated supplies. Stowaways. More

than a hundred monsters trying to land on the beach."

"The attack in the jungle," I added.

He nodded.

"You think someone is gearing up for a big attack."

"It seems that way."

"Any idea who?"

He rolled his shoulders.

"Well, don't worry. You've got the Grae sisters on the job."

"That sounds ominous."

I tossed him a grin as I sauntered for the main area. "Don't worry, Spot. We'll keep you safe. After all, you can't seduce me if you're dead."

13

·)·)·)·⊙·(·(·(·

I loved having the final word. After dropping that statement, I winked and left Bane with his jaw on the floor—pity it wasn't his shorts. With a swing to my hips, I emerged from the bedroom to find my siblings admiring the view from the window.

"I can't believe I'm in South America," Frieda mumbled. "I wondered why I kept trying to put razors on my grocery delivery list."

"You should get laser hair removal. Way better," I chimed in.

Dina glanced at me. "You should have called."

"I spent a few hours in the jungle before hitting civilization. By then, I knew you were already in the air."

"What can I say? I was craving some heat. Besides, Frieda was a mess."

"Was not," Frieda mumbled.

"You were the one who called me shrieking, 'That bitch accepted!'" Dina shook her hands in exaggeration.

Frieda pursed her lips. "You're an ass." Then to me. "What did he offer?"

"My choice of any treasure I wanted from his vault."

"What's your top pick?" Dina asked.

"I don't know. I haven't seen his stash yet."

Both my sisters blinked at me. Dina said, slowly, "You accepted a job without seeing the actual payout."

"Well, we already know I'm getting sex out of it. Plus, some kind of expensive treat? Sounds like a win to me."

Dina shook her head. "Since when do you think with your crotch?"

"Um, have you seen my new boss?"

"His friend is cuter," muttered Frieda, causing me and Dina to stare at her in shock.

It led to me saying, "He needs a seer to help him with something."

The "No," Frieda uttered came a little too fast —and pink-cheeked. Before I could ask if she'd seen something about John and her, someone knocked at the door.

I took a position with a nice line of sight, still armed with the shitty gun I'd taken off the attacker in the jungle. Dina flanked me, ready to fling magic, as John, without any kind of precaution, answered the door. A hotel worker in a bright flowered shirt stood there with a cart covered in domed dishes.

They wheeled in the cart, took the tip offered, and left just as my boss emerged fully clothed.

John headed for the coffee pot, and I couldn't help but chirp, "Pour a plain cup for me." John had just grabbed the urn by the handle when Frieda pounced and knocked it out of his hand.

The java spilled on the floor, and John, with a mouth open wide in shock, yelped, "What did you do that for?"

My sister bit her lip before murmuring, "It was poisoned."

We eyed the puddle and then the food.

"All of it?" John sounded almost mournful.

Frieda took her time eyeing everything and shook her head.

John grabbed an orange. "Surely this is fine."

"I see someone poking it with a syringe."

The way that orange dropped and John scrubbed his hand was almost comical.

Bane growled. "I think it's time we left."

Frieda cleared her throat. "You should avoid the yacht."

"Dare I ask why?"

"It's going to sink."

He sighed, and I frowned. "I thought these people wanted to keep you alive."

"Apparently that's changed."

Ooh. Even more of a challenge.

I rubbed my hands together. "All right then, we need a new plan to return to the island." I eyed Frieda. "Chopper on the roof?"

A negative toss of her head. "Explodes."

"Any suggestions on what we can use?"

Her nose wrinkled. "Not really."

It was Dina who poked her. "Liar. What did you see?"

My sister sighed. "Sea-Doos."

"Really?" I brightened. "I love those things." They were like snowmobiles for water.

"I don't," Frieda grumbled.

Bane snapped his fingers. "The marina has rentals. I assume they're okay."

Despite her downturned lips, Frieda bobbed her head.

"Let's head out. Stairs okay?" He once more addressed my sister, and I tried to not have a jealous fit. What happened to me being the one looking out for him?

"There will be an attack in the stairs, but it won't impede us or cause any harm if Enyo goes first."

"On it." I went to leave, only to have Dina clear her throat. "Want your bag of stuff first?"

I glanced at her. "You brought my travel kit?"

She pointed to a colorful bag on the floor. "I stashed it with my things so that the spell would keep security from noticing it."

"Sweet!" I dove on the bag and just about crooned to my set of throwing knives, the holster that held two guns, and my thigh sheath. Even better, a set of my clothes, including shitkickers. I didn't put them on. A Sea-Doo was no place for leather, buckles, and steel-toes boots. I'd change into them once I got to the island.

Armed, I headed for the door, Bane at my heels. "Where do you think you're going, Spot?" I tossed over my shoulder.

"To handle the threat."

"That's my job. You're supposed to stand back and look pretty while I protect you."

"Like fuck," he snapped.

"You know if you had an HR I'd probably have to complain about your attitude."

"Don't like it? Quit."

"Ha, you'd like that, wouldn't you? Then you wouldn't have to resist my allure."

He snorted. "You really think highly of yourself."

"I do." I stalked out of the penthouse into an open-air hall with just the single door. At the far end was a set of stairs.

Some people liked to move slowly and cautiously. Personally, I hated giving people that much warning, so I ran, my bare feet making little to no sound. I kept my hands free, mostly so that once I reached the stair railing, I could grab it and vault, dropping down an entire landing, surprising the pair of thugs waiting.

One provided a soft landing—for me. He, on the other hand, cracked something on the way to the floor. Oops. I popped to my feet, and my fist lashed out at his companion before he could bring his weapon around. My balled hand got him in the nut sac, and he crumpled as I rose. My grip on his hair and a knee to his face dropped him on top of his friend just as Bane arrived.

His glare said, *Don't do that again.*

As if I'd listen. I smiled. "Clear."

"Not quite," he growled as shots fired from the first floor. They pinged and ricocheted, one of them coming close enough I almost lost some skin.

"Oh, more makes it a competition. I'm already at two. Try and keep up, Spot." I vaulted over the railing and tucked as I dropped in and surprised a group of four. Nothing like landing in their midst to make them hesitate to shoot.

My leg snapped out and swept the nearest ankles. A knife in another hand took care of a few tendons but resulted in some shrill screams.

Bane arrived in time to drive a meaty fist into the face of the guy aiming his gun at me. The fellow dropped hard.

"One for you. Good job," I taunted, his scowl well worth it. I moved from the heap of bodies to peek around. "I don't see any others."

"We're clear to the rental place," Frieda announced as she arrived, tucked behind John's scholarly back. Dina floated down using magic, which had her skimming over the bodies and blood spatter.

Her lips pursed. "Once again, I am reminded why your closet is full of dark clothes. What ever happened to your lessons on killing via pressure points?"

I shrugged. "Not as satisfying."

She sighed. "I am also reminded of why we don't work together often." At the sight of my bare feet, she brought forth her bag. "Let me get your boots."

"Hold on to them for now. If we're going Sea-Dooing, then I won't want their weight."

"We should move," Bane snapped. "Follow me."

The dumb Warden tried to take the lead, as if he wanted to be target practice. I jogged ahead and took point. While Frieda would warn us if she could, she didn't always see things that might affect. It paid to be vigilant.

I found it amusing that John hovered close to her, as if she were some fragile flower in need of coddling. I might be the assassin in the group, but my mother ensured we all knew how to protect ourselves. While reluctant to use violence, Frieda could mete it out if she had to.

Alas, we made it to the weather-beaten building by the beach without issue. Blame the many tourists making it harder for would-be assassins to attempt an attack. Maybe I'd get lucky. After all, they'd brazenly come after us at the hotel.

While Dina bargained, using Bane's credit card, I stood on the quay with my boss, who stared out over the water.

"Worried?" I asked.

"No."

I glanced at him. "Are you lying to me?"

"Surprisingly, I'm not. I hate to admit you seem rather capable."

A noise escaped me. "It is why you hired me."

He rolled is shoulders. "It's more than that. You

don't get flustered. You think on your feet. You all do."

"We didn't have a choice but to become adept. Mom insisted we learn how to use our gifts." And she didn't believe in coddling us while doing so. Just look at how she'd left poor Frieda in the cemetery overnight to see if she could contact the dead. She couldn't, but boy did I have fun making her think they were coming after her. A few moans, some rattling chains, and a smoke machine totally worth the price.

"Your mother is alive?"

"Yes, but she's off on some kind of retreat. Has been for a few years now. Something about communing with her goddess." At times, I couldn't help but feel abandoned. No more traps to get the pulse pounding when she came to visit.

"Who does she serve?"

"Apate."

"The goddess of deceit?" He sounded surprised.

"Yeah. She's never been the baking-cookies type of mom. She was more the pot brownies, cigarette-smoking type."

"And are you a disciple of Apate as well?" he asked. "Should I be worried about betrayal?"

I snorted. "No, Apate is not who blessed us. Which peeved off my mom. She's tried for years to find out which god it was. No one recognizes the mark left on us when we got our powers, though."

"Wait, you have an actual physical mark?" At my nod, he added, "Can I see it?"

"Why, Spot, I knew you'd ask me to undress sooner or later." I winked.

Before he could grumble, Dina stalked toward us, looking annoyed. "The guy only has three Sea-Doos available, meaning we will have to double up."

"Good, because I hate driving," Frieda declared.

A lurking John overheard and immediately made an offer. "You can ride behind me."

I expected my sister to argue, but she nodded.

Which left me, Bane, and Dina. No way was I putting her behind my boss.

Still, I appreciated it when he stated, "You two should ride together seeing as how I probably weigh as much as both of you."

"You'll go slightly ahead, and we'll follow. That way I can watch for threats coming for you."

The life vests impeded my ability to draw my weapons, which drew curious gazes when I tried. But this far south, no one said a thing. I ditched the vest in favor of movement.

The Sea-Doos were bright green and white, fairly new, and powerful. I couldn't wait to get out on the water. I stashed as much as I could inside the snug storage compartment, and then I straddled the seat. Dina clambered on behind me, her life vest making it harder for her to get a good grip. She settled on holding on to the loops of the shorts I'd borrowed from Bane. A glance showed the petite Frieda actually sitting in front of John, his arms long enough to bracket her and still be able to drive. I wondered at the pink in her cheeks. Sun or something else? I hoped for the latter. My sister could use a fling in her life.

With everyone settled, we took off. The Sea-Doos skipped over the waves, the wind whipping at my face, the sun beating on my skin. Dina held tight and uttered little yelps, not enjoying it as much as me. Bane understood though. He weaved and jumped the swells, his body moving and guiding the machine with a fluidity I admired.

A good thing I watched because otherwise, I might have missed the large shadow moving under him. A submarine? The shape didn't seem right. Whale? Could be. I had no idea what to expect in these waters.

The scream of the machines made talking impossible, so I throttled up and moved to flank Bane. He glanced over and saw me. I took one hand off the handlebars long enough to point at the water.

His gaze followed, and I saw the moment he realized we had company. Could be just some kind of aquatic creature out for a swim, but assassins didn't live to an old age unless they were paranoid about everything.

Bane swerved, and the shadow under the waves followed. He cut back, and the thing swimming with us began to rise.

Time to act. I yelled, "Dina, drive."

If she'd been human, me suddenly standing up to dive would have tossed her ass in the ocean, but my sister had magic. So when I hit the water, she used her power of telekinesis to steer the Sea-Doo away from me.

I stroked through the clear ocean toward the rising behemoth. Not a whale as I'd suspected, but a barnacle-covered turtle of a monstrous size. I managed to grab hold of its carapace as it surfaced and headed for Bane. It moved swiftly through the water, its mouth opening wide, ready to chomp.

Not on my watch. I scrambled across its back, staying hunched over to grip with my hands as my bare toes dug into the crusty growths. My flesh stung from the tiny cuts and abrasions. Here was to hoping the turtle didn't ooze any poison.

Once I reached the giant turtle's head, I pulled a gun and fired. Might as well have spat, as its thick skull didn't seem to feel the bullet that lodged. It gained on Bane, who kept looking back.

I needed to find a more vulnerable spot.

"Sorry, big guy, but you should have stuck to a seafood diet," I murmured as I fired into its squishy eye.

The reaction proved instantaneous. The giant turtle heaved, throwing me from its back. I would have been fine when I hit the water, only its flipper smacked me upside the head and put me to sleep.

14

The Warden

·)·)·)·)·⊙·(·(·(·(·

BEING ON THE SEA-DOO BROUGHT A SENSE
of freedom Bane had been lacking of late. Jumping
the swells, swerving tightly, and creating wakes all
reminded him of the simple pleasures he'd been
missing.

But that joy came crashing down when Enyo
indicated something in the water. The size of the
creature shadowing them daunted, especially since
he couldn't count on his feline to fight. He did have
a gun holstered to his side, but he knew shooting
into the water would be a waste of a bullet.

When the turtle surfaced, he found himself
stymied as to how to handle it. Enyo had no such
problem. She surfed its back and attacked it, got

tossed in the process, but succeeded. The blinded turtle sank under the waves. As did Enyo.

He kept waiting for her to reappear, and when she didn't, he didn't hesitate. He took only a second to smack the kill switch on his machine before diving off its seat. He sliced into the water, heading in the direction he'd last seen her.

The clear water let him see her sinking, her body limp, a thin trail of blood a cause for worry. Not because he thought her injury serious, but it would draw predators.

He kicked with his legs and pulled with his arms as he stroked for her, his lungs tight as he went deep. He managed to tangle a hand in her hair, enough to stop her descent and drag her to him. With one arm around her, he then pushed to the surface, propelling them quickly into the air. As he blinked water from his eyes, he felt the steady thump of her heart, and it reassured.

"Watch out!" He heard the shrill cry and had only enough time to throw himself backwards as the injured and now very angry turtle returned, its gaping maw barely missing his legs.

He floated on his back with Enyo, knowing he couldn't outswim the beast.

"Goddamn it, you leave my sister alone," screamed the sister named Dina.

The air pressurized, crackling with power. He

had only enough time to turn his head before the explosion. Chunks of meat—turtle meat to be exact —rained down on the water and him.

A glance showed the witchy sister straddling the Sea-Doo, the glow of magic fading from her hands, but she'd not worked alone. John also dropped his raised hands. Their combined power had been enough to save him and Enyo, but they weren't out of danger yet. Bane kicked for his Sea-Doo, heaving Enyo over the seat before climbing aboard. He managed to get her tucked against his chest then yelled, "Let's go." Because this much chum would draw predators who might decide they wanted a living snack.

The Sea-Doos whined as they raced away from the carnage. Only moments later, fins began popping up, heading for the feast.

There were no more distractions as they caught sight of the island, which shimmered in the distance before solidifying, knowing its master came home.

Cradled against his chest, her legs draped over his, Enyo stirred, mumbling, "This position would work better if you weren't wearing pants."

"Do you ever not think about sex?" he grumbled in an effort to ignore how the suggestion affected him. Why did she have to make it so hard— literally hard—to resist her?

159

"Who doesn't enjoy a romp after defying death?"

"Speaking of which, most people would say thanks for saving their lives."

"Just say the word and I will orally thank you until you can't remember how to speak."

"You're insane."

"So I've heard." She squirmed against him until she could see over his shoulder. "What happened to the turtle?"

"Turned into soup by your sister and John."

"Nice. I know she's been working on a combustion spell."

"Dare I ask why?"

"Never know when you'll need to blow up some shit," was her completely serious reply.

He slowed the machine down. "We're almost to the island."

"Let me see." She just about dumped them as she twisted and turned until she faced forward, putting her buttocks firmly against his groin. Her new position shoved him back on the seat, making it impossible for him to drive—which she knew. She grabbed the throttle, and he had to hold on to her as she sped for the rocks.

"Careful," he cautioned.

"Never," she laughed in reply. Despite this being her first visit, she saw the channel that provided safe passage to the dock and eased them up to its side before grinning at him over her shoulder. "Fun ride."

"Says the woman who needs stitches."

Her bloody temple had begun to clot, but the gash would need some help to heal properly.

"Bah. Dina will fix me up."

"She can heal?"

"Not exactly, but she's good at patching my injuries." Enyo grabbed hold of the dock and vaulted onto it before reaching for the rope to tie off the machine. She helped her sister Dina dock next, while John handled his machine and deposited Frieda.

A pair of the mercenaries Bane had hired from the Arcane Guild of Fighters stood watching. He headed for them and, once in earshot, asked, "Any trouble while I was gone?"

"Nah," stated the older of the AGOF soldiers named Kyle. "Your mermaid's pretty efficient. Only one sea monster made it to shore, but the ogre took care of it."

"Good. It will probably get worse over the next few days. By the way, we'll need someone to return these to the town." He indicated the Sea-Doos. "Also, someone needs to check over the yacht and helicopter, as they've been tampered with."

Kyle nodded. "I'll let the master chief know so he can send a team."

"Thanks. Notify him I'll want a debrief on events while I was gone, but no rush. I'm going to handle my guests first."

Enyo stood at attention within earshot. She looked at everything, not in awe like most, but with narrow-eyed suspicion.

He joined her and murmured, "Anything wrong?"

"This place is wide open."

"As opposed to...?"

"I would have thought, given what I've learned so far, that you'd have some kind of a walled fort, but your town"—she swept a hand—"this dock, everything I can see has absolutely no defenses."

"Because most of the time it's unneeded."

"Until it is," she pointed out.

He wanted to argue but couldn't. Would it have made a difference with his parents had his father put more defenses in place? "Maybe after this eclipse, you can advise me."

She cast him a glance. "Why, Spot, are you asking me to stay?"

"Uh..." Yeah, he had no reply.

Enyo glanced at her sisters, who leaned over the dock to talk to Melisandre, the mermaid who'd surfaced to say hello to the newcomers. "You weren't kidding about the mermaid."

"Would you like to meet her?" he offered.

"Hell yeah." She didn't wait for him but sauntered over to say hi, reaching down to shake a hand, which amused Melisandre.

"You are the Warden's new champion?" Melisandre trilled.

"Yup. Although I'm surprised he needs me. I hear you're quite the warrior," Enyo praised.

No surprise, the mermaid preened. "Thank you."

Enyo left her sisters and demanded Bane take her to the beach caves to introduce her to Sam. By the time they left the ogre, she had him wrapped around her finger. Most likely because she'd spent some time admiring and exclaiming over his nail-studded club.

She would have explored the town next, but he put his foot down. "You can't go wandering around with a bloody head."

"It's just a flesh wound."

"This is not a Monty Python joke. In real life, it's called an infection waiting to happen."

She sighed loudly. "Fine, take me to your castle."

Her sisters had gone ahead with John, who knew the way and which quarters were meant for guests. Basically, all the rooms but Bane's. The place didn't look all that impressive from the outside, given a good chunk of the castle was carved into the mountain of rock, most likely added after the first Warden found himself tied to the portal underneath.

Rather than see its age and grandeur, she noted its defenses. "This causeway isn't narrow enough. It makes it hard to defend." She glanced over the sides and tsked at the slopes. "Way too easy to climb."

"What would you suggest?"

"Knock it out entirely and build a drawbridge."

"No moat?"

"Don't be silly. Then people could swim over. Much easier to ping them off when they're trying to climb."

Her logic did make sense.

As they continued the trek, she felt a need to talk. "You said earlier your parents sent you away before the events that led to their deaths. Why, if there'd never been any big trouble before? Couldn't they have just plopped you in a secure room with a guard? And what about the army they assembled? Those fighters I saw in your dream must have come from somewhere. That shows planning and forethought. Not the kind of thing you throw together last second."

"The Warden always assembles a fighting force

before the hybrid eclipse. It's just not usually used much."

"Then why send you off? What made them think that time would be any different?"

The decades that passed had him straining to recollect, only to shake his head in defeat. "Honestly, I didn't really pay much attention. I was a teenager more concerned with getting laid at the time."

"It appeared coordinated. Meaning someone assembled that attack. Was that person ever found and eliminated?"

"The wizard who tried to kidnap me, who killed my father, died that day by my hand."

"And you're sure he was the one in charge?"

Again, he lacked a reply. "I assume—"

She interrupted. "You know what they say about assuming."

"I've gone through two eclipses since then with barely any issue."

"And yet you've already told me this time feels different."

No denying it. "The lead-up to the event has been a lot more violent than previously. The incursions happening sooner than usual."

"How long has the island been in this spot?"

"Almost three years."

She whirled on him. "I thought you said it usually parked itself a year before the event so as to remain unnoticed."

"Usually. I'll admit I was surprised, but it didn't prove to be an issue until recently."

"You said your bodyguard died six months ago from bad soup. I wouldn't call that recent."

"That was the first death. The second one was a fluke accident."

"Fluke how?"

"Marcus went deep sea fishing with an expedition and fell overboard. Unfortunately, the sharks got him before the crew could drag him back aboard."

"Yikes," she stated.

It still brought a pang, seeing as how Marcus had been a close friend for more than a decade at that point and stepped in when he saw Bane had need. "You saw today how dangerous the ocean can be."

"That wasn't a random attack, and you know it."

"I know that now. But it took two temporary bodyguards from the guild also dying under mysterious circumstances to realize the problem."

"You've lost four bodyguards?" Her brows lifted. "How am I just finding that out?"

"I didn't count them since I wasn't with them when they died of, again, plausible causes."

"There you went assuming again."

"You can leave if you want." He offered her an out. An unwilling guardian wouldn't be of help.

She snorted. "Please. You do realize this is what I do, right?"

"Do you ever wish you could change your lot in life?"

"And become some boring chick with a regular job? No thanks." As they reached the castle gates, the metal frame as thick as his arms, the bars only slightly thinner, she shook her head. "These are pretty but completely useless. A portable Sawzall will cut right through those bars."

"They might find that challenging with someone shooting at them from the other side."

Her lips quirked. "That works, but you should think of electrifying them when they're closed."

They went through the small courtyard full of sunshine into the castle proper. Despite being fitted with electricity fed by solar panels, hurricane lamps filled with oil remained affixed to the walls.

She glanced around. "Where's the chamber with the pillar?"

"Before we continue the tour, you're getting cleaned up. I'll show you to your room."

"Not so quick. I'm sleeping with you, Spot."

"No, you're not. You need rest, and we both know you didn't get any last night."

"Can't keep you safe if we're not in the same room."

"Didn't matter this morning, or have you forgotten how easily your sisters got to me despite us sharing a space?"

"Bah. I knew they were coming."

"You knew?"

"Told you, we're linked."

"And if they'd killed me before asking questions?"

"I would have stopped them before that happened. Now where's the master bedroom so I can see what I'm working with?"

"It's in the tower." He led the way up to the topmost floor with three stories of winding, narrow stairs, which she approved of.

"A person could hold off an army in this space." Her arms had to bend when she touched both sides of the wall. "Must be a bitch getting furniture up here."

"Most times we hoist it up to a window."

She groaned. "How big are those windows? You have heard of grappling hooks, right?"

"Would you feel better if I said there are bolted shutters?"

"Slightly. Bars would be better."

"I thought you said bars could be sawed."

"They can, but the noise doing so gives you

time to act."

The solid wood door to his room remained locked in his absence and, given it was keyed to only him, took his hand pressed against it to open. He let her inside the airy and bright space.

"I thought you said there were shutters," she muttered as she cautiously moved around, glancing under chairs and the table, even kicking those empty spaces with her foot.

"Will I get in trouble if I admit I don't use them often?"

"It's like you want to make things easy for your enemies."

"Or I don't want to live like a prisoner."

She whirled to stare at him and shook her head. She pulled her gun, frowned at it, and tossed it on the bed. She pulled a pair of knives and hit the floor, rolling quickly under the bed. A squeal sounded, and a moment later, she emerged, dragging a limp lizard with a defined set of teeth and a spiked, barbed tail.

He gaped. She held it up by the scruff. "And this is why you should at least have screens with an electrical current running through them."

"I can't believe I didn't smell it." He still didn't.

"Guess your nose can't always be trusted." She went to the window and dropped the lizard intruder before saying brightly, "When's lunch?"

15

·)·)·)·⊛·(·(·(·

WHILE I'D NEVER ADMIT IT LOUD, BANE'S castle impressed. Yes, I'd busted his balls on its security, but at the same time, it wasn't all bad. The wide-open window thing was an issue, though, which I'd just proven, but he'd not been pissy about me being right.

Instead, he sat me in a chair by a window and went to get a first aid kit. Usually, I would have handled the boo-boo myself, but quite honestly, I liked having him touch me. Waking up cradled against him after that oversized turtle took me out proved more than pleasant. If it hadn't been for my promise to let him seduce me first, I would have totally taken advantage by nibbling on that sweet neck of his.

Alas, I'd made a vow, and I would stick by it. I just hoped he didn't keep me waiting too long because the longer he played hard to get, the more I wanted to jump his bones.

With a sexy stride that rolled his hips and reminded me of the vee hidden under his shirt, Bane returned with a damp cloth and a box stamped with a red cross. He set the kit on the table and began sponging my temple. Gently. Softly. As if I were delicate.

Snort.

"You'll never get any dirt out if you don't scrub a bit," I couldn't help but chide.

"I know what I'm doing."

He removed some butterfly closures and ointment from the kit. His firm pinch pulled the cut together. He smeared and then plastered me, stepping back and declaring, "That will do, but keep it dry when you shower for at least a day or two."

"Sweet. Thanks for the patch job. Now, you're going to accompany me to find Dina so I can grab my shit. I am ready for my own clothes." I pulled the damp shirt from my skin.

"Not so fast. We only handled the biggest wound. Let's see those hands and feet." He knelt and took the latter, making me wonder what he thought of my callouses. Soft soles could kill a person in the field. I purposely walked barefoot in places guaranteed to toughen them up.

He said not a word as he cleaned and rubbed a lotion into my not-so-tender-tootsies. My fingers, rough on the tips, and my equally thick palms didn't need much help. The minor abrasions were quickly cleaned, and yet his touch lingered as if reluctant to lose contact. Or did I imagine it? Maybe he didn't get the same tingles I did when we got close. I thought it more likely he did, given how he avoided my gaze. Odd from a usually direct man.

Once finished tending to my minor boo-boos, he packed up the stuff and said, "Let me find you something dry to wear." He headed for a doorway that must have led to a closet since he emerged with a shirt.

"Oh, hell yes." I thought nothing of stripping mine. After all, sharing one room with three sisters meant I'd never been a prude. Besides, I wore a sports bra. You'd have thought it fancy lingerie the way Bane froze in place, staring. I plucked the shirt from his grip and put it on. "Let's go."

"Where?" he asked, his eyes still focused below my chin. I wasn't the type to be offended. Let him admire because that might lead to him finally making a move.

"To find my sisters, of course."

"Knowing John, they're probably the floor

down from us. Why don't you go meet up with them? We'll reconnect later. I have affairs to tend."

"Not without me, you don't. So, let's go check in with my siblings, and then we'll go deal with your shit."

The annoyed pinch of lips warned he would argue. "I don't need you being my constant shadow."

"Yeah, you do. So don't argue."

"You seem to think I work for you."

"As your bodyguard, I get to tell you what you're allowed to do."

"I'm safe in this castle."

"There was a monster under your bed."

"Bah, I played with bigger as a cub."

I blinked. "Seriously?" And yet I'd never encountered any. How did that track? It seemed odd in retrospect how casually he treated monsters and magic, whereas in my tiny world, it was just my sisters, mother, and her small circle of friends, who'd certainly never discussed the arcane with us. Suspicious now that I knew.

"I've been able to shift since birth."

"Wait, you ran around as a kitten?"

He nodded.

I couldn't help but laugh. "That is the most fucked-up, hilarious thing I've ever heard."

"It's natural for a shifter."

My lips curved. "When I was a baby, I ate, shat, and slept. I didn't inherit my gifts until I hit my teens. In a funny coincidence, I was born during an eclipse, which repeated on my sixteenth birthday, which happens to be when me and my sisters gained our powers."

"If I were a man who analyzed omens, I'd question three eclipse-born being here for the hybrid event coming in a few days."

"It does seem like a rather rare coincidence," I agreed.

"More than rare. Impossible. Yet here we are." Spoken almost musingly before he added, "Let's go find your sisters."

"Why the abrupt change of mind?" I just couldn't accept the easy win.

"Because I am honestly not in the mood to take on this fight. Let's go."

I'd won. I should have been happy he'd listened, but instead, I glared at his back. Why didn't he fight more? A man like him, used to being in charge, should have had more to say and bluster.

He didn't look over his shoulder to see if I followed him down the stairs. Probably smelled me with his kitty nose. As he predicted, my sisters had the room right below, having chosen to share one with a king-sized bed.

At our entrance, Dina held out my satchel of

toys and clothes, knowing I'd come for it. Frieda sat cross-legged on the bed, hands on her knees, eyes closed as she centered herself. She'd once told me new places overwhelmed with the futures of everything she came in contact with. Like how a vase would fall, crack, get glued, then fall again. Get tossed. Useless information to know, and yet she couldn't always stem the tide.

"Nice digs," I commented, peeking around. The whitewashed furniture had colorful accents: bright-hued pillows, a blue comforter that matched the rug.

"Guess we should say thanks for the tropical vacation. Can't wait to work on my tan." Dina held up the skimpy bikini she'd pulled from her seemingly bottomless bag.

"Hardly a vacation," mumbled Frieda, coming out of her trance. "The violence that's about to occur is ridiculous."

"You saw something?" I asked a little too enthusiastically. Dina often joked my middle name should have been Psycho. I didn't disagree.

"Don't have to. Surely you feel the ominous portent in the air." My sister's nose wrinkled.

"Is that what that awesome feeling is?" I inhaled deep and grinned as Frieda sighed.

Dina snorted. "Only you would be excited by that."

"A little bit of excitement is good for the soul," I quipped. "Since you guys are settling in, I'm going to keep Bane company while he conducts important Warden business."

"We don't need you babysitting." Dina waved me off. "I'm sure I can find something to keep us busy."

"I am not building sandcastles or sunbathing," Frieda warned. "And before you argue, I saw how those ended. With you stomping the first and laughing, and me burning in the second."

"Since when can you see your own future?" I exclaimed.

"I still remember what happened the last time we went to the beach," Frieda spat with a dark look at me and Dina.

"We were playing Godzilla and Kong. Of course, we had to smash." Like duh. I snapped my fingers. "While we're on the subject of the past, John was wondering if you ever saw it."

"No. Is that even possible?" Frieda queried, lips pursing.

"John seemed to think so. You should ask him."

"I wouldn't want to bother him," Frieda demurred.

I clucked.

She glared.

I clucked again. Yes, I knew she was an introvert. I also knew she hated being alone even as she insisted on it. Making her put herself out there a bit here and there did her good. This John fellow didn't seem half bad, and I'd seen how Frieda blushed in his direction. Maybe she'd get laid. That'd be the bonus on top of my payment.

A flat-toned Frieda said, "While you're being annoying, your boss is escaping."

Bloody hell, he'd slipped into the stairwell. "I'll see you later." I fled after the boss. Bane moved quickly, but I had no problem catching up.

"You should have stayed with them," he grumbled.

"And miss out on your grumpy personality?"

"It's not grumpy to want some privacy."

"It is when your life is in danger. But tell you what, I'll let you use the bathroom in peace."

"Praise be," he said dryly.

On the main level of the castle, we found a giant, gray-haired man talking to a guy in combat gear.

"That's Lorcan, the master chief," Bane confided as we neared. "He's in charge of the army I hired."

"Is it me, or does he look part bear?" I joked.

"Because I am," boomed the big man. Lorcan turned to us, showing an impressive set of whiskers.

"You must be the assassin the Warden went to test. I take it you passed."

"Piece of cake. He should have had me wrestling you instead of that gator if he really wanted to make it a challenge."

Lorcan blinked at me before guffawing loudly. "Funny girl."

A sexist bear. Awesome. I couldn't wait to put this Lorcan in his place. Would he be the type to cry for his mama?

I'd challenge him later. For the moment, I stuck to business. "How many people do you have with you?" I asked.

"Thirty-seven."

I frowned. "That doesn't seem like much."

Lorcan puffed his chest. "My troops are the best. Worth five times their number."

Doubtful. Most people couldn't fight multiples at once. "They've engaged in warfare before?"

"All of them are field seasoned against both humans and monsters."

"You've fought monsters?" I couldn't even believe those words came out of my mouth.

"Yes, as well as cleared out nests."

"This is going to be an invasion. Much different since we have to defend rather than attack," I pointed out.

"I know what I'm doing, bossy girl."

Oh, the challenge would be coming soon. He'd pay for calling me girl. He was right about the bossy part, though. "Hard to tell your level of competence given the slackness I saw from the docks onward."

"How many battles have you been in?" Lorcan groused.

"Depends on what you consider a battle. But to give you an idea, I've killed more people than John Wick at this point."

Lorcan's brows almost fell off his forehead. "Damn."

I smiled. "And that was without me losing a dog. Imagine now what will happen if I do get mad. Now, back to your lack of soldiers..."

"I am just following his orders." Lorcan dumped the blame on Spot.

"Keep in mind we have limited space to house them," Bane murmured.

"Soldiers are used to roughing it. Although I'd hardly call camping on the beach with this mild of weather rough. Try sleeping in a tree with one eye open for poisonous caterpillars, blood-sucking bats, and hungry panthers." That had been an epic camping trip.

"My soldiers will prove themselves," Lorcan promised.

"Guess we'll see," I replied.

Before the bear man could get pissy about my doubt—and allow me a chance to put him in his place—Bane stepped in. Spoilsport.

"Tell me what's happened while I was gone."

I tuned out as Lorcan relayed his report on the easily repelled monsters that had been poking around. Despite me busting his balls, the guy seemed to know the basics. He spoke of the patrols he'd set up, the motion sensors he'd placed, and other safeguards to warn of incursions.

He and Bane had a good rapport. When we left Lorcan, I murmured, "Surprised you didn't take him on as your bodyguard."

"I used him temporarily," Bane admitted.

"And?"

"He snores like a bear. Even outside my door I could hear him."

"You mean I won because I don't keep you awake?"

He shrugged. "A man needs his sleep."

"Aha. I knew there was a reason."

"Reason for what?"

"For you not seducing me yet. It's because you hate missing out on sleep. And this close to your big day, you're worried about being tired, because we both know when we do have sex, it's going to be epic and neither of us will get much shuteye." A statement that teased with a wink.

Rather than grumble, he offered me a sly smile as he said, "I wouldn't need all night long because I know what I'm doing."

Panty-creaming words. But did he follow up with proof? Nope.

"What do you want to see next?" he asked as we reached the main level, a vast, arching space with balconies and slitted windows that let in light and so many possibilities. Did he have a throne room? What about his vault? Ooh, his armory.

I eyed the various archways before finally asking, "Which way to the pillar?"

"Follow me."

It started with a closed wooden door opened not with a key but a metal mechanism that he moved in a pattern to unlock. That led to a set of winding stairs heading downward that reminded me of the dream. I eyed Bane's broad back as we descended. I couldn't help but feel sorry for him. How horrible to have been a spectator to his own parents' deaths. And then to be unable to escape it. Tied to the scene of tragedy. Forever cursed himself.

"Stop it."

"Stop what?" I asked.

"I don't need your pity."

"It's not pity to think it must have sucked."

"It did," he stated, pausing before a locked gate made up of bars spaced close together. It blocked the entrance to a tunnel. "This is the way down to the cavern."

"I kind of figured. How many people can open this door?" I asked as I eyed it for a key-hole or another of those puzzles that would un-lock it.

"One. It's keyed to only work for the Warden." He put his hand on those strange bars, and without hesitation, it swung open.

"What kind of metal is it?" I couldn't help but eye the strange glint on the bars. Black, silver, and gold all in one.

"Unknown. But I can tell you they can't be cut."

"I take it you've tried?"

"With every blade I could find on the market. After my parents died, I tried to destroy this place. I wanted nothing to do with the curse that took them."

"And yet here you are still, doing your duty."

He grimaced. "Only because I worry about let-ting loose something worse."

"Let me ask, if you're the only one who can open this door, why not leave it locked and go on vacation during the eclipse? Wouldn't that foil your enemies?"

"If only it were that easy. There is a reason my father let my mother die. To remove his hands during that crucial moment would have allowed the portal to open."

"Wait, so this portal opens on its own, every hybrid eclipse?"

"Yes. Only the Warden can keep it from releasing what's on the other side."

"Seems like a shitty curse to put upon someone," I remarked.

"It is." His lack of argument deflated any sassy reply.

As he led the way, the tunnel and the staircase we passed through were clean of the blood that once stained them.

"That gate that only you can open, why not close it once you're inside? No monsters and people with weapons able to follow means you could put your hands on that door without issue."

"According to the few witnesses left, the monsters took my parents by surprise. They had to fight their way inside, the monsters, some of them human, with them every step of the way. They couldn't get the gate shut in time."

"Meaning, get you in place early with super gate shut and we're golden."

"I hope it's so easy," he muttered as we entered the vaulted cavern from the dream.

My neck craned to take it all in. The soaring ceiling. The hole overhead letting in sunlight. I pointed. "How come the monsters don't come in through that hole?"

"Because that hole doesn't exist. Not in this world at any rate."

"Er, what?"

"I've been over every inch of the castle and the mountain it's built upon. There is no opening to this cavern. When it's dreary and raining outside, there is sunshine pouring in."

"What about nighttime?"

"There is no night."

"Wild." Knowing magic existed didn't prepare me for a place that took it to the next level. "Would it be okay if we showed my sisters this place? Dina will be fascinated." And who knew what Frieda would see.

"Why not?"

"Maybe you'll get lucky, and they'll break the curse." I approached the walls with their strange markings. "What does it say?" I asked, tracing my fingers over the etchings.

"I wish I knew. I've taken snippets of it to scholars around the world. No one's ever been able to translate it for me."

"I have that issue with my mark too. Mom tried to figure out which god blessed us, but no one's been able to read it."

"Can I see?" he asked.

"Go ahead." I whirled and lifted my shirt to show him the tattoo I'd received on my sixteenth birthday. Unlike the large, intricate circle with petals that I'd gotten intentionally, my original mark was pale white, almost like scarring, only there were no ridges to it.

"It's glowing," he murmured.

"It is?" I tried to crane to see but then held my breath as his fingers lightly skimmed the flesh of my lower back.

"Do you know what the symbols look like?" he asked.

"Yeah." We'd taken pictures of them and studied them to no avail.

He removed his hand. A shame, because I'd enjoyed the calloused touch. "You'll want to see this."

Bane's long stride moved him away from me toward the pillar I'd yet to inspect. I headed for it, and a shiver hit my entire body. More concerning, the tattoo on my back heated, and as it did, a section of symbols on the pillar ignited in a pinkish glow that parted my lips.

"Holy shit," I whispered. Because there, carved in stone, were the same marks as on my back.

16

The Warden

-)·))·)·⊗·(·(·((·

THE MOMENT ENYO REALIZED THE MARKS on her flesh matched those on the pillar, she bolted, leaving Bane behind. He didn't move, partially because of his own shock. For one, he'd never seen the pillar glow other than during the hybrid eclipse. Secondly, what were the chances he'd connect with someone with the same indecipherable symbols? Might be time to believe in omens.

In short order, Enyo returned with her sisters, the three of them alike and yet not. Enyo had their fine features, but with more height and muscle tone, fit for a warrior. Dina, the witch, had an aura and an arrogance around her. And then Frieda, the frailest of them all, with her own quiet strength.

The sisters clustered in front of the pillar that

glowed, three sets of repeating symbols, one for each woman. Of concern, no eclipse in sight but still he wondered if he should have his hands on it. Was the portal opening early? He'd never seen it react like this before.

Dina gestured to him. "You, Warden fellow, what's the history of this thing?"

The query lifted Bane's shoulders as he joined them, hands stuffed in his pockets. "No history. None that I've found at any rate. The previous Wardens tended to hand down their knowledge orally."

"How inefficient," Enyo remarked.

"Annoying I would have said, because you're trusting in memories that we know can be faulty." He'd long lamented the fact no one seemed to have any knowledge for him. Vague references in history texts from around the world had been all he'd gleaned. Even his father hadn't told him much be-cause, at the time, he'd assumed someone else would take on the role of Warden since Bane made it clear he'd leave as soon as he became eligible for college.

"Tell us everything you know," Dina commanded.

"This place is old."

"Duh." Enyo's helpful remark.

He continued as if she'd not spoken. "From

what I've been able to gather, it's been around at least five hundred years, if not more."

"What makes you think that?" Frieda had her hands tucked behind her back as if afraid she'd accidentally touch something.

"We came across a graveyard, of sorts. A handful of graves to be exact. The remains were exposed after a nasty storm took down a tree."

"Who were they?" his new bodyguard asked.

Again, he could only shrug. "No idea. They didn't have any tombstones with names. Their clothing had long since decayed. I had the bones analyzed, and we ascertained their age at death. Two males well into their sixties, one female approximately thirty years of age, and one child."

"Could they have been the first Wardens?"

"The males, yes, but doubtful of the other two."

"That's sexist," Dina huffed.

"Don't blame me for it. I would love to have seen this gift go to one of the fairer sex. Alas, the recipient of the Warden's role doesn't seem to have a choice."

"How is a Warden chosen?" Enyo's sister Dina had all kinds of questions.

"That is a mystery. It's thought they have to be in proximity to either the outgoing Warden or the portal, but that distance can vary. My father wasn't even in the room when the previous Warden died. My uncle Rupert, along with a few others, were by Warden Gregor's bedside, hoping to inherit, and yet, it skipped them for a visitor to the island."

"This Warden power chose you upon your father's death," Enyo stated before her sisters could ask. "How did you know? What did it feel like?"

"As if I got hit by lightning. Needless to say, I wasn't happy about it and did my best to rid myself of it." His lips turned down. "I went to every witch and wizard I could find. A range of them that covered a good dozen different gods. None could help me."

"Because they cannot interfere in another god's blessing." Frieda's quiet claim had them all looking at her.

Dina took a soft tone as she prodded her sister. "Do you see something?"

"No, but I can feel it. Pain. Violence. Betrayal." Frieda's fingers trailed on the column, and Bane stiffened as the whole thing flared bright yellow. Her head tilted back, her eyes rolling back, and from her came a voice that wasn't hers on a chilling breeze.

"Lies began the treachery. Jealousy kept it captive. Love will set it free."

Frieda snatched her hand away as quickly as her head snapped upright. She hugged it to her chest. "I don't like this place. Something very bad happened here."

"No shit," Bane muttered.

"How is it the same writing on this column appears on our bodies?" Enyo pointed. "It can't be a coincidence we've been drawn here."

"I want to run some magical tests on it," Dina murmured, putting a hesitant hand on the column.

"Magic doesn't work. Or at least, that of my friends doesn't. And it should be attempted with care. Meaning, I need to be in the room," Bane cautioned. "I don't want that portal accidentally opening."

"Did it ever occur to you that maybe whatever was locked away is either dead or no longer dangerous? Centuries is a long time," Dina intoned, staring at the column.

"Finding out could be the thing that ends the world," he pointed out.

"You're basing this on some dudes from hundreds of years ago, a time when they didn't bathe because of bad spirits, thought weather events were god-related, and women were only good for popping out babies. You said it yourself, there's nothing actually concrete written about this place, and yet you've dedicated your life to it," Dina prodded with some uncomfortable truths.

"The fact demons and monsters came here and

killed my parents is a good reason to keep whatever is inside there locked away."

"There are some who advocated doing the same to me." Enyo's soft murmur. "Put a boy in the hospital for trying to grope your sister and they all act like you're unfit."

"Can we go somewhere else to discuss this? It's probably time for lunch," he stated, wanting to leave this haunted place. The many pointed questions had him uncomfortable. Did the Warden do good by keeping the portal closed? Did he guard it for nothing?

Enyo led the way out of the cavern with her sister Dina, the two of them with their heads close together as they discussed how to proceed with some testing. Frieda remained close to Bane, her expression haunted.

"You look troubled," he muttered.

She glanced at him. "You would be, too, if you knew this was the place your sister was going to die."

17

⟩⟩⟩⟩·⊙·⟨⟨⟨⟨

FRIEDA MUST HAVE SAID SOMETHING TO MY boss because he not only emerged from his dungeon hideout wearing a mighty scowl he also tried to fire me.

Bane pointed to the main castle door and barked, "You need to go."

"Where?" I asked. "What's next on the tour?"

"Nothing, because you and your siblings are leaving."

Given Frieda slunk off, I had a feeling I knew why he had a change of heart. "Let me guess, Frieda told you I was going to get hurt."

"Die, actually. So, you need to leave."

"No."

"Did you hear me?" he growled.

"I did. I'm choosing to ignore you."

"Why?" he bellowed to my back, seeing as how my nose followed the smell of food.

"Because this wouldn't be the first time she's seen me croak," I offered over my shoulder as an explanation. "This isn't even the tenth time. I lost count long ago."

"This isn't funny," he snapped as he followed. "I won't be responsible for your death."

"You won't be. I take responsibility for my actions." And personally, I thought more people should too.

"Except you wouldn't be here if not for me," he pointed out.

"Don't be so sure of that. I'd say the fact your special pillar and my tattoo have the same kind of language makes it clear destiny meant for me to come here. Can't wait to see what happens next." I really couldn't. You know those signs that said don't touch? Guess who liked to poke.

"Why aren't you more worried?" He kept haranguing as I paused outside a kitchen that wafted delicious aromas that made my mouth water.

"My job is dangerous. Always has been. Always will be. But this time it has the added bonus of maybe giving me some answers on why my sisters and I were chosen. What our purpose is. Because why else mark us and give us our abilities unless we were meant to do something extraordinary?"

"Doesn't the lack of choice in the matter bother you?"

I shrugged. "I could if I let it, but what would that accomplish? Do you like being angry at fate?"

"Some of us would prefer to not be a puppet."

"Then learn to cut the strings. It's what I've done. It's why I can hear my sister's predictions and change them."

"Change them how?"

"By finding out the details around my death and countering them. Someone using fire? I wear fire-retardant clothes and an ointment. Gas? I wear a mask. Gonna be shot at, don't be in that spot in the first place."

"You make it sound easy, but what if there is no way out? I don't want you to die."

"Why, Spot, I'm tickled you care, but really, I'll be fine. Unless you don't feed me, and then all bets are off." I made a beeline for the chef, a rotund woman in a stained apron who had florid cheeks from the oven. She saw my hungry ass coming and quickly tossed some yummies on a plate. Smart lady. Always serve the hungry assassin.

I thanked the cook and carried my meal past the dining room to sit outside in the courtyard in the sun. Like literally sat down cross-legged on the stone since no one thought to put out any chairs. How a person lived in paradise without a proper outdoor patio baffled.

The boss, with his own plate, followed, frowned at my seating arrangement, and then joined me. "I can't believe you're being so blasé about a prediction of your death." He just wouldn't let up.

"Would you prefer I was hysterical and clinging to you desperately?" I took a bite of food and grunted in satisfaction. Breaded fish that crunched and gave me a salty bite. Fried plantain for some sweet, and sticky rice to fill me up. So fucking delicious.

"Have you no sense of survival?"

"I didn't make it to almost forty by being reckless."

He eyed me. "You *are* reckless."

My lips curved. "Fine, how about I'm not suicidal. I don't intend to die. After all, I can't collect if I'm dead."

"If you want payment, then let's go to the vault right now. Choose whatever you want and go."

"If I leave, my sister's prophecy won't come true."

"Exactly."

"I meant the one about us becoming lovers."

He choked on his rice. The spew of it made me

sad. What a waste of good food.

I pounded him on the back because a body-guard should protect her client, even from asphyxiation when he forgot how to chew and swallow.

Once he could control himself, in a voice gruff from coughing, he muttered, "So if we have sex, you'll leave?"

"Are you trying to imply you're so bad at it that I won't be able to look you in the face the day after?"

He gaped for a second before recovering. "What will it take to get you to leave? Treasure? Take everything you want. Sex? Fine. Let's go up to my tower and get it over with right now."

My lips curved. "Mmm, angry sex. Tempting. Alas, I don't have time right now. Maybe later when we're snuggled for the night."

"How can you not have time?"

I put my plate aside and stood, rolling my shoulders. "Because right now I need to do my job. Get inside."

"Why?" He frowned at me but still joined me in standing.

"Because we're about to have company." I lifted my head to eye the sky and the dark spots approaching.

His gaze followed mine. "Most likely a flock of seagulls."

"Those are much too large and dark. Not to mention, I feel a tingle." A strange sensation that rippled along my flesh and adrenalized. I usually felt it before a fight. I glanced at him. "How good are your snipers?"

"I don't have snipers," he admitted. At my surprise, he added, "Never had a problem from the sky before."

Rather than rebuke the man who knew about monsters for being shortsighted, I grabbed him by the hand. "Let's get a better vantage point."

No point in leaving him behind since I knew he wouldn't sit out the skirmish. Best to have him close by.

"I don't suppose you keep rifles stashed on the parapet," I asked as we went up some narrow stone steps to the wider passage on the wall. I had some knives and a pistol, not the best weapons against an aerial attack. Short-sighted of me. Given the only two approaches to the island were by sea or air, I should immediately have thought to set up some kind of sky surveillance with Lorcan and his soldiers. I wondered if they had any bazookas. One of my favorite toys.

"The weapons are in the armory and gun vault."

"Which is kind of useless in an emergency," I remarked as I glanced around to see if those approaching specks only came from a single direction or all at once. The panoramic view from the parapet proved breathtaking. Blue ocean waters sparkled as the sun's rays danced on its surface. The little town spread below the castle was quaint with its whitewashed stone exteriors and gray clay roofs.

"It's called ensuring children don't have access."

"Or you could, you know, teach them the proper usage and respect for weapons." I pivoted to see what the best vantage spot would be. I pointed. "Stand there and don't move."

He eyed the open spot I'd chosen. Far from any concealment, it painted a lovely target on him as a matter of fact. "Dare I ask why?"

"I can't take them out long range with this pistol, so I need them to get close. If they're aiming for you, it will make it easier."

He glared at me. "You're using me as bait?"

"You're the one who wouldn't go inside. Now stop yipping and get ready."

His idea of "get ready" involved suddenly shredding his clothes to become the leopard. Big kitty with massive paws. Maybe he would be a little useful.

"Here they come," I warned softly as I lifted my gun-wielding hand.

And then, because I had a perverse sense of humor, I hummed my favorite battle song.

18

The Warden

AN ANNOYED BANE OBSERVED THE approaching aerial menace.

Bait, indeed. As if that weren't affront enough, she began to hum. Loudly. And not just any song. "Ride of the Valkyries."

He had to admit it kind of fit. The race toward a fray. The adrenaline firing the blood. He paced in the short space, waiting for his chance to battle.

Enyo got a head start with her pistol. She fired at the albatrosses, massive birds of the ocean that usually didn't fly in such huge numbers. But in good news, while big and annoying, albatrosses had no arcane abilities, meaning when one got near, he could reach up and swipe it from the sky, sending feathers and birds to crash to the ground below.

"Three for me, one for you," sang his body-guard, keeping count.

Enyo appeared to be having a grand time, with impeccable aim given the bodies that kept dropping, thinning the cloud. She soon had help sniping, as Lorcan hustled a few soldiers into the courtyard to take shots, reducing the not really dangerous attack. If it was even an attack.

Perhaps the birds had reacted to something environmental. Animals had been known to flee before a natural disaster. Shit, should he be looking to the horizon for a tsunami?

When Enyo started swearing, he feared the worst, especially since she yelled, "Big mother fucker coming in from the southwest."

He pivoted, albatross hanging from his powerful jaws. He didn't see a mega wave but a massive blot in the sky. Bigger times a hundred compared to what they fought.

"The birds are a decoy," she screamed down to Lorcan. "I need a bigger gun!" She then held out her hand as if one would magically appear.

To his credit, Lorcan didn't hesitate. He ripped a rifle from a soldier and, with a mighty heave, sent it arrowing for Enyo, who, of course, caught it. In a fluid movement that must have taken years of practice, she had that gun up to her cheek, sighting on the big-ass bird winging their way.

Bang. Bang.

She fired, and yet the approaching threat didn't falter. Rather, the air in front of it shimmered.

It had a deflecting forcefield, making it arcane in nature. It took a few shots before Enyo cursed and came to the same realization. "I can't penetrate its shield." She glanced down at Lorcan. "Suggestions?"

Lorcan, not Bane. He couldn't help but be insulted.

"Draw it down here where we can surround it." The "we" referring to Lorcan and the soldiers stripping to shift.

Before Enyo could ask him to move his bait-like ass, Bane leapt from the parapet, landing lightly as all felines did. The AGOF soldiers fanned out from him, leaving him as a tempting target for... He blinked, but the realization didn't change. A roc—a massive bird thought to be myth—neared enough for him to make out details. The sleek feathers with a metallic hint made him wonder if they would act as armor. The wide-open beak showed serrated edges for shearing, and the claws were big enough to pluck up an elephant, or so the legends claimed. Definitely big enough to grab one leopard and fly off.

He didn't see Enyo on the ground or the parapet, which didn't ease his mind. What was she plotting?

No time to find out. He coiled and readied for the plunging roc, which came at him, talons extended. Before it could reach him, a soldier—already shifted into a lion—leapt with his jaw wide open and claws unsheathed.

The screech of those nails dragging across metal made everyone wince, and the attempted chomp failed, as the feathers did indeed act as an impenetrable carapace. Not that it stopped the other shapeshifters from attacking as the roc alit. Bodies leaped for the oversized bird and were flung off, batted by wings. Even the ruffle of the tail feathers had enough force to toss. The soldier unlucky enough to get caught in that powerful beak died swiftly, his body cut in two.

Bane didn't flee, despite having no idea how to fight this monster. It had to have a weak spot. He just needed to spot it.

Was it the eyes? Even as he thought it, he saw a bullet deflect from the surface of an orb, which answered that question. The neck and underbelly both had those tough feathers shielding them. Could he perhaps wedge a paw between to slice?

Seeing the many bleeding cuts of those attacking he could only assume there were razor-sharp edges on the plumage.

Fuck.

He darted as the beak came at him, doing its best to make him lunch. He dodged then flattened his body to the ground as a wing swept over, looking to shear him in half.

Over him charged a massive bear, a shifted Lorcan in a berserker rage throwing himself at the roc. He managed to hug and hold it in place for a few seconds, long enough for a chain to suddenly lasso the roc around the neck. Bane gaped in disbelief as Enyo dropped from above, hands wrapped in fabric, holding that chain and using it to anchor herself as she hit the roc's back.

The bird didn't like it one bit and screeched, bucking its body, trying to fling off the person daring to ride it. But Enyo held on as the roc suddenly leapt into the air, flapping its wings, taking them into the sky—where Bane couldn't follow.

He and everyone else in the courtyard could only watch as the roc got smaller and smaller, as Enyo got farther and farther away.

His stomach knotted. Was this when she died?

He only barely noticed the arrival of Enyo's sisters. The seer was on his left, wringing her hands. The witch to his right, the air around her vibrating as she drew on her magic.

There was a collective gasp as they saw a small speck detach from the larger one.

Enyo fell.

A second later the roc exploded, and as chunks of the bird fell, John yelled, "Take cover. Those feathers can still kill."

Bane realized the danger wasn't over.

He also didn't move. Couldn't as he watched Enyo plummeting, arms and legs wide like a starfish, as if that would slow her descent. He couldn't look away despite knowing she'd splat.

And it would be his fault.

He shouldn't have drawn her into his problem. Shouldn't have—

"Stay under the shield," John shouted as a shimmering blue disc appeared in the air overhead. Not wide enough for the entire courtyard but big enough for those remaining outside to stand under it as the first of the debris began to hit and ping, sharp feathers dropping hard enough to embed into the stone of the courtyard.

But wait, how was it the carcass arrived before Enyo?

Dina held her hands out in front of her, glowing a deep magenta. A paler version of that magic surrounded Enyo.

By the time his bodyguard landed on her two feet, smiling with triumph, Bane was livid and thought nothing of shifting to bellow, "What the fuck is wrong with you?"

19

·)·))·)·⊙·(·((·(·

MY BOSS STOOD NAKED IN THE COURTYARD, bristling with tension and anger—also a bit of worry, apparently. His fists hung clenched by his corded thighs, and yes, my gaze strayed to his dick. In my defense, even in repose, it commanded attention.

"Well?" he barked.

"You're welcome," I replied.

Not the right one, apparently, because he yelled, "My room this instant!"

Off stalked my boss, and I stared at that sweet ass of his. So did my sisters, and as a knife found its way into my hand, I debated how much I really loved them.

Luckily neither moved to follow Bane, and I

tempered my killer instinct—a.k.a. jealousy. New one for me. Usually, I only coveted weapons—of which, technically, Bane was one. A living, beautiful beast made for sleek battle.

Dina made a moue of distaste as she glanced around. "Nasty mess."

"Yeah, well, a grenade down the gullet will have that effect." Lucky for me, I'd slipped one from my kit, as I liked to always have one on my person. Never knew when I'd want to blow up shit. As for the chain I used as a lasso, I borrowed it from the mechanism for raising the portcullis. They'd have to fix it before they could crank it open again.

"I can't believe you jumped on its back! You could have splatted," Dina chided.

"Bah, I knew you wouldn't let me fall too hard." It wouldn't be the first time Dina floated me out of a bad situation. There was that time I got caught on the 32nd floor of a building when it caught on fire. Good thing Frieda had sent her to give me a magical hand. I glanced at my seer sister to add, "Thanks for making sure I had a rescue."

Frieda chewed her lower lip. "Actually, I didn't see this happening. We just heard the commotion, and Dina insisted we check it out."

"Bullshit. I know you told Bane I'd die."

"I did," Frieda answered with a shrug. "But it wasn't today or in this courtyard."

"Then where?" Because forewarned meant I could prepare.

Her gaze drifted to the ground as if she could see through it to the chamber below. "It's going to be a bloodbath."

While nonchalant about my own welfare, I did love my sisters and so had to ask, "Do I need to send you and Dina away?"

"We survive what's coming. You don't." She paused before blurting out, "He lets you die because of that stupid portal."

Just like his father. I tried to not feel a twinge of disappointment. After all, we'd not known each other long. Why would I expect him to save me over the world?

I pasted on a bright smile. "Good thing I know better than to count on a man to rescue me. I prefer to save myself."

"There is one surefire way to make sure you don't die," my sister stated.

"I'm not leaving."

Frieda held her chin up as she said, "Actually, I was going to suggest you eliminate him."

I arched a brow. "You do realize he hired me to save him not murder him?"

"Why do you care if he lives or dies?" Frieda cried out, drawing attention from those that had shifted back. Lorcan cast us a sharp glance. Want to bet he'd heard every word?

"I care because it's my job, and you need to trust me. I'll figure a way out. I always do."

"I say we let that door open and see what comes out," was Dina's sly suggestion.

"I'd rather not be known as the triplets who started the apocalypse." Then again, infamy had its perks.

"Enyo!" The bellow came from a window far above. "Get your ass up here."

I smirked. "Gotta go. The boss is calling." Would he try and spank me? I'd never been into that type of thing, but there was always a first time.

Leaving my sisters, I headed inside and up the stairs in the tower, hoping Bane hadn't gotten dressed. Alas, I entered the room to find him wearing shorts, his skin moist where he'd run a cloth over it. At my arrival, he stopped pacing and glared.

A mighty glare. It warmed me in places he probably didn't mean it to.

"You bellowed, Spot?"

"What you did outside—"

"Saved your life and that of your hired soldiers. You're welcome. In better news, I'm not even going to charge you extra for it."

For a second, he seemed at a loss for words.

Then they came rushing out on a growl. "You were reckless."

"Brave."

"What if your stunt had failed?"

"But it didn't."

"What if it had?" he insisted.

I shrugged. "I wouldn't be alive to care then, would I?"

"Argh." The inarticulate cry sent him pacing.

"Delighted to know you care, Spot."

"More like it's too close to the eclipse to replace you," was his dark reply.

At that, I chuckled. "No shit. I am unique."

"And insane. What possessed you to jump on its fucking back?"

"Nothing else seemed to be working. I thought about trying to toss the grenade into its open beak, but had I missed, there would have been friendly casualties."

He stared at me. "I fucking hate it when you counter with logic."

My grin widened. "Does that mean I'm forgiven?"

"No. And don't ever do that again."

"Yeah, we both know I'm not going to promise that, and we also both know I will totally do it again. Think that roc had any pals?"

At that, he shrugged. "Who fucking knows.

Rocs were supposed to be a myth. And it's not the first monster we've seen of late that isn't supposed to exist."

"And they're all coming to see you," I mused aloud. "Could someone be doing something to encourage them to attack, or do you think the portal in your basement is sending out an extra strong vibe this time round?"

He shook his head. "I don't know. How does anyone control monsters? Why would the portal be stronger now?"

"Maybe the magic holding it together is getting weak. Or it has a time limit. Or"—I ticked off fingers—"the stars and planets are doing some ultra-alignment in time for the eclipse. Or—"

He cut me off. "I get it. There could be myriad reasons for the sudden influx. My problem is, how do we keep people safe? Much as it pains me to admit, if you'd not taken care of that roc, the casualties would have been much higher."

"Why, Spot, I do believe that was almost a thank you." I beamed. He scowled. "Oh, don't be so grouchy about the fact I think well on my feet. As to protecting your people, anyone who doesn't want to fight should be sent to shore."

"I can't see many of them leaving," he admitted with a sigh. "Maybe some of the old and the very young, but everyone who lives here knows what the island is about."

"Even they must be having issues with the increased danger this time round. Give them the option, if only to make your conscience clear. Then tell Lorcan we need more Guild soldiers. There should be snipers on the parapets watching the skies. Weapons stashed all over in plain sight for people to grab and use. Pity we don't have time to seed the waters with mines."

"I doubt Melisandre would like that."

"I'm sure she'd like even less to be overwhelmed and eaten," I pointed out, which caused him to grimace. "If they can swarm from the skies, they could do the same from the sea."

He rubbed his face. "I hate this."

"Want some cheese with that whine?"

That burned away the pathetic for an angry retort. "Easy for you to mock. You're not the one trying to keep anyone from dying."

"Um, kind of trying to keep you from an untimely end," I pointed out with glee.

"A demise they shouldn't have to share."

"You're not responsible for their choices, and yes, it is them choosing to live here. What you can control are *your* options."

"What options?"

"Well, there's dying, which I don't recommend.

There's breaking the curse, which might be a bit tricky given the late date. Doing your best to protect the door. Or you could say fuck the door, fuck the job of Warden, and let the portal open."

"Unleashing destruction on the world."

"Are we sure that's what would happen? You said it yourself, there is no history about what's been imprisoned, and like I said before, you don't even know if there's still anything alive on the other side."

His lips pinched tight. "Releasing it disrespects the sacrifice my parents made."

"Has holding on made you happy?"

"No. But what else could I do when the task fell to me?"

"You do realize when you die the curse will pass on to someone else."

"Yeah, but at least it won't be a child of mine. I made sure of that."

The finality of his tone had me quipping, "Did you get the big snip?" My fingers scissored in the air.

"Yes."

I laughed.

"I fail to see the humor."

"It's more like a chuckle of solidarity. Given I'm not into the whole baby thing, I had my tubes tied in my twenties to the shock of my sisters."

"You don't want kids?"

"Nope. I'll spoil any nieces and nephews I get, and I'm not a dick to the young by any means, but that whole maternal thing? Not my scene."

"You're an unusual woman, Enyo."

"Ditto, Spot."

He stared at me.

I stared right back.

A strange moment of connection that he ruined by turning away and clearing his throat to say, "I should be supervising the cleanup."

"I wonder if roc tastes like chicken. Think your cook can salvage any of the meat?" I mused aloud.

He choked. "Um. Yeah. No."

"If you're going to play outside, you should take one of these." I dug into my kit and offered him a grenade while tethering a fresh one to my belt.

He eyed it like it would explode. Had he never used one before? "Pull the pin and count to five to make it go kaboom!"

"I doubt we'll see another attack today."

"I agree, which is why I'm letting you go mop up the courtyard while I talk to Lorcan about stepping up the defenses."

He took the grenade with reluctance. For now. Once he blew something up, he'd change his mind.

Nothing like an explosion to get the blood pumping.

We left his room together and yet far apart. Him returning to stew in his guilt and misery, me wondering why I cared how he felt.

Not much was said the rest of that day. While I worked with Lorcan— who had whole new level of respect for me given I'd shown myself to be even more berserk than him—tightening security, I kept an eye on the boss as he handled a mop and pitched in to help clean.

My sisters had vanished, but John wielded a hose. I'd seen him trying to approach Frieda earlier, only to watch in entertainment as she fled as if he were the devil. I'd have to ask her later what that was all about.

Dinner proved to be a raucous affair. Surviving death tended to do that. It pleased me to see no one drank alcohol. Today's attack showed just how alert we all needed to be.

A few soldiers were missing, getting in some sleep before their shift tonight. We would be watching the skies and the beach. By "we" I meant Lorcan and his crew. I had my own task, watching over my mopey boss. He remained quiet during dinner and barely ate. How hard it must be to live with burden of being responsible for the whole world.

The man took things way too seriously. It led to me drawing Dina aside after dinner to murmur, "I don't suppose you've taken a peek at the boss to see if he's under a spell."

"You mean the whole Warden thing? I've looked."

"And?"

"He's definitely got something inside him," Dina confirmed.

"Can you remove it?"

"Depends. Do you want him alive after?"

Meaning no.

My disappointment must have shown because Dina added, "But I've only just begun to check things out. Tomorrow, I've got plans that involve a better look at the pillar in that chamber. Maybe we'll learn something."

Ah yes, the secret cavern that Frieda said I'd die in. I wanted to scout it more too. Maybe plant some traps, stash a few weapons.

Speaking of whom, I spotted my sister just outside the dining area, staring at a painting. I made my way to Frieda, my steps loud so as to not startle her.

She didn't turn as she spoke. "Go away."

"Don't be so grumpy, French fry." The nickname I'd given her when we were young that I used when I wanted to antagonize.

"Do you know how hard it is to look at you knowing you're going to die in a few days?"

So dramatic. Also, not the first time she'd said the exact same thing. "I'm not croaking. Not yet."

At that claim, Frieda whirled, her expression tight with anger. "I should push you off this wall right now and save the future the trouble."

"We both know you won't."

"It would be easier than spending the next few days agonizing over your death."

"Surely there's a future where I don't get taken out."

"One out of hundreds. One!" she yelled.

"See. It's not a done deal. Any clues as to what I have to do in order for that one to happen?"

Her lips turned down, sadness in her gaze. "The impossible."

"Bah. Never say impossible. Come on, spill."

"You have to make the Warden love you more than his duty."

For the first time in my life, I felt a real chill because she hadn't exaggerated. I wasn't the lovable kind. Fuckable, yes. Dependable, definitely. Fiercely loyal to those I cared about, always. But lovable? Only my sisters ever managed that, and they struggled with it at times.

I spotted Bane leaving the dining room. Rather

than reply to her statement, I offered a brusque, "Gotta go. The boss is on the move."

"I love you, Yo-yo," Frieda's retaliation for French fry.

It led to me grabbing her for a quick hug and whispering, "Don't lose faith."

I'd lost Bane from sight, but instinct led me to the tower stairs. My steps quickly brought me in range of my boss, who not once acknowledged my presence as I shadowed him. He appeared still caught inside his own head, the crown of it dipped in thought, his shoulders hunched, a man on the verge of defeat despite our victory against the roc.

I was on his heels when he entered the bedroom. He whirled fast enough I almost ran into his chest.

His hands shot out to steady me even though I didn't need it. My lips curved into a smile. "Nice reflexes."

Rather than reply to my compliment, he grumbled, "There will be no sleeping in a chair tonight."

I glanced at his shuttered windows. At least he'd been listening. "If you insist." I eyed the divan by one of those shuttered openings. Some armless thing that would barely fit half my body.

He growled. "We will share the bed."

My lips tilted. "Now you're talking."

"Get your mind out of the gutter. We're not having sex."

"Me thinks thou doth protest too much." I sauntered from him.

"What are you doing now?" he snapped.

His sharp tone might have had to do with my ass in the air. I peeked at him coyly over my shoulder. "Checking for monsters under your bed." I also scouted his closet and the bathroom, where I closed the toilet lid and placed a deodorant atop. If it got knocked off, I'd hear it. I did the same thing for the shower and sink drain. Not all threats came in big packages. Some of the deadliest things in the world could fit in the palm of your hand and needed only a single drop of poison to kill. I would know. I'd used more than one venomous spider in my work.

Done with my rounds, only the divan remained to slide in front of the door.

"It's locked, and only I can open it," he stated from the bed. He'd stripped and gotten under the covers while I went around securing the room.

"Nothing wrong with being overly cautious," I chirped as I eyed the shuttered windows. Not much I could do for them. At least anyone trying to enter via those openings would make a racket.

Only a single lamp remained lit as I went to the empty side of the bed. One gun went on the nightstand. Another under the pillow. A third remained strapped to my ankle. A shotgun lay just under the bed. A rifle hid in the closet. I had a few grenades stashed around the room, part of my afternoon prep. I'd also gotten Lorcan to sprinkle more weapons and ammo throughout the castle.

Despite my teasing of Bane before, I didn't get completely nude. Shirt and bottoms came off, sports bra and panties remained on, along with my throwing knives' sheath. While some people didn't mind fighting nude, I hated it when my boobs jiggled. And getting guts caught in my short pubes? Kind of gross, even for me.

Bane said not a word as I climbed into bed with my mini arsenal.

The light went out, the silence in the room broken only by our faint breaths and the slight rustle of fabric.

Still too energized for sleep I said, "What a day. Gotta say, being with you doesn't lack for excitement."

"Does anything ever bother you?" he replied.

"I'm not one to waste my time on the negative. It accomplishes nothing. You should try it sometime."

"Hard to be positive with everything that's been going on."

"I know a way to make you smile," I teased.

He sighed. "Good night, Enyo."

"Night, Spot."

With that, he turned away from me, choosing to be alone. Then again, I shouldn't judge. If it weren't for my sisters, I'd have no one either.

No dreams that night. I slept like a rock. Unusual for me since I tended to wake at every slight noise or movement. Apparently, my body trusted Bane. Trusted him so fucking much that when I woke in the morning, I had a moment of surprise as I realized the fucker was gone.

20

The Warden

BANE KNEW HOW TO MOVE QUIETLY. Partly it was due to his feline heritage and partly because, when young, he used to like sneaking up on people and yelling, "Boo!" The screams gave a boy with not much to entertain him a cheap thrill.

He'd spent a portion of the night awake. Worried. Horny.

It didn't help Enyo gravitated toward him in her sleep. She didn't kid about being the big spoon. She smothered him, a leg flung over his thigh, face buried against his back. Cuddling. A new thing for him, and he didn't hate it—with her, at least.

There were many things about Enyo he liked, even as he wanted to shake her until she agreed to leave. How could she hear about her own death and

221

not want to escape it? Enyo acted as if it were a joke. Her blasé attitude only made the knots in his stomach more painful while, at the same time, he couldn't say why he cared.

They barely knew each other, and yet he felt a comradery with her, a pull, a sense of rightness, desire, and, worst of all, hope. A hope he wouldn't spend the rest of his days alone that reminded him that he'd also promised himself to never drag anyone else into this nightmare. Not full-time at any rate. A promise easy to keep, until Enyo.

Now he fought the urge to drag her into his arms and kiss those lips. Strained to not turn in her spooning embrace to wake her with soft caresses. Clamped his mouth shut lest he say things that couldn't be taken back.

It didn't help his cat wanted to rub his scent all over her. Maybe pee outside the door to warn other males to stay away.

When morning hit, he reluctantly eased himself from her embrace. He moved with a stealth she would have admired, lifting the divan from the doorway and setting it down without the slightest thump. His door never made a single squeak as he fled.

Like a coward.

He went looking for breakfast and ran into the

witchy sister sipping a tea as the castle cook prepped breakfast.

Dina eyed him over her cup. "You look like you had a rough night."

"It's been a stressful few weeks."

"And here I thought it was for another reason." Half her mouth quirked.

"I am not fucking your sister." The vulgar term slipped from Bane, and her husky laugher showed no sign of offense.

"You will. Anyone with eyes can see you're both attracted to each other, but I'm going to guess you're being stubborn."

Was it that obvious? "I've got too much going on to get distracted."

"And yet you're already preoccupied because you won't give in to your desire."

He opened his mouth to deny, only to realize it would be a lie, so he changed the subject. "When do you want to investigate the hidden chamber?"

"This morning if possible. The sooner we start, the better."

"Do you think you can do something about the portal?"

"No."

He blinked.

She offered an enigmatic smile. "The kind of

magic described is way beyond my abilities. From the sounds, it leads to another dimension."

"You've dealt with them before?"

"Yes and no. My bag? It's got a tiny alternate dimension inside, bought for a hefty sum from a wizard. So it's not a far stretch to imagine one created as a prison or even leading to another world entirely. Have you ever spoken to someone who knows how to create and tether another plane of existence?"

"No." Because he'd assumed his situation unique.

"You should because they might provide insight."

"I'd prefer they shed me of it entirely," he grumbled as he poured a coffee and joined her.

"If you could rid yourself of the role of Warden, what would you do?"

"I don't know."

"Surely you've thought of it," Dina prodded.

Actually, he didn't dare because that path led to depression. "No, because being Warden is for life."

"It doesn't have to be."

"You're right. I could die." He rolled his eyes as he took a sip of the strong brew.

"That's not the only option. You could just let the doorway open."

"Now you sound like your sister."

"More like I'm capable of looking at this from a selfish viewpoint. If it were me, I'd be questioning why I'm devoting my life to a cause that no one can explain to stop a danger no one can describe."

"I do it to protect the world."

"Some would say the world can protect itself," Dina pointed out.

"Maybe I don't want the deaths it would cause on my conscience."

"Ah, I see now. You'd rather be a martyr. My bad."

His brow creased. "No. But—"

"But what? Explain to me how you're not throwing yourself on the sword, so to speak. And for what? You won't get a reward or even thanks. On the contrary, by the looks of it, you've closeted yourself off from attachments."

"Not true. I have friends."

"But no lover. I talked to your people. You don't have relationships."

"Because I won't be an asshole and impose this life on someone else."

She rolled her eyes. "Did it ever occur to you that someone might be willing to share that burden? Of course not, because then you couldn't play a tiny violin while being the grouchy curmudgeon."

In that moment, she reminded him of Enyo, who also accused him of something similar.

"It's not fair to ask someone else to join me in my curse."

"Nice of you to make that decision and assume a lover would be so weak. Do you think your mother ever regretted marrying your father?"

"No." The love his parents had for each other had been deep, but not deep enough for his father to forsake duty.

"I wonder if it's because you've yet to fall in love," Dina mused.

Before he could say never, Enyo found him.

"I swear, it's like you want to get eaten by monsters!" Enyo's sudden rebuke didn't take him by surprise because he'd felt her coming.

Felt. Not heard or smelled, but sensed in a way he'd never experienced with anyone else. He refused to acknowledge what it meant. "Not my fault you slept in."

"Stealthy fucker," she muttered, snaring a coffee. She joined them at the table, grunting, "Morning," to her sister.

"Someone woke up on the wrong side of the bed," Dina sassed.

"Don't start with me," Enyo grumbled. "I'm not in the mood."

"Given you're in such delightful spirits, I'm thinking I should borrow the Warden and check out that pillar again," Dina suggested.

Bane expected Enyo to insist she tag along, but she nodded. "Go ahead. I've got some stuff I want to check out."

Stuff? What stuff?

"Awesome. Ready?" Dina directed the question at him.

"In a second." First, he shot Enyo a dirty look, because she probably deserved it, then grabbed a muffin still hot from the oven, along with a few strips of bacon. "Let's go."

"Try to not unleash any monsters," Enyo chirped after them.

"That won't be a problem, will it?" Dina asked with a hint of concern as he led the way.

"Only if they make it inside. But I don't think that's happened yet, and even if they did, the gate is closed and only I can open it."

Said gate, the first and only barrier to the cavern, clearly intrigued Dina. She ran her fingers over it and murmured, "This metal isn't from this world."

"It would explain why it can't be cut." He placed his hand on it, and the door unlocked.

The lack of a key led to her adding, "Whatever magic power it holds isn't one I can see either."

"You see magic?"

"In a sense. It's more like an aura, sometimes even just a tiny wisp of color."

"I've never heard of that." Then again, he didn't often discuss magic with his friends.

"From my studies, I know it's a rare skill. Most wizards and witches need to cast an actual spell to see it."

"You seem well informed. Enyo didn't seem to know much about the arcane."

"Because Enyo's always been more interested in the physical fight. Given my particular gift, I've sought out knowledge, only to realize for every tidbit I discover, there's even more left to find. It doesn't help people are well hidden and reluctant to share information."

"What have you heard about other realms of existence?"

"Just what the movies have taught me," she offered with a laugh. "If we're being honest, you and John know more about magic than me. That said, the advantage I bring is that I have no preconceived notions. I've found those raised with the arcane and its rules are closeminded when it comes to experimenting. They don't know how to push boundaries or query outside the box."

"Aren't you worried about setting something off because of that lack of knowledge?"

"Not really. According to Frieda, I'm not going to die for a long time."

It made him wonder if he should ask the seer

what she saw in his future. Then again, knowing might be worse.

They entered the chamber and his stomach knotted at the sight of the pillar. The blood spilled on the dais had long since disappeared. Literally. He'd left that chamber, stumbling in his grief, not stopping until he knelt in the courtyard, tears streaming as he screamed to the sky. By the time he recovered enough to return and start the removal of the bodies, there was nothing left.

No blood. No corpses. Nothing. The grave he gave his parents held nothing but a box of memories.

He tried to pay attention as Dina ran her fingers over the faintly glowing pillar. While she circled it, examining it from every direction, his mind strayed.

What was Enyo doing?

What if they were attacked and she needed his help?

When would he see her again?

It turned out to be within the hour. While Dina scribbled in a notebook while occasionally squinting at the pillar, Enyo arrived along with Frieda. They appeared to be arguing.

"...you're being crazy."

Enyo sighed. "Oh, would you stop it already? We both know I'm not going to listen. But do you know who would love to talk to you? John."

"I can't help him," Frieda insisted.

"You haven't even tried."

"Maybe I don't want to." A stubborn reply.

"Well, just because you're content to be a blob who does nothing doesn't mean I am."

"Rude!" Frieda huffed.

"Then do something about it."

One interesting thing—not related to the fight —how the entire pillar began glowing brighter at their arrival. Enyo did have a point when she said something bound them. What did it mean for the upcoming eclipse?

It took him a second to notice Enyo had a rope with a grappling hook and another second to realize what she intended.

"What are you doing?"

She kept swinging the rope back and forth while eyeballing the hole high overhead. "I wanna see where it goes."

"Nowhere."

"How would you know? Have you looked?"

"I told you I searched the island for it."

"Yadda. Yadda. I know that. I also know it's gloomy as fuck outside, and yet that's shining bright." She jerked her head upward, indicating the hole. Her sisters joined in looking overhead. "I want to see what's going on up there."

"Sticking your head in some weird magical hole

for a peek isn't a good idea," he stated, crossing his arms.

Enyo glanced at Frieda. "Do I die today?"

Her sister's lips flattened, but she managed a gritted, "No."

The smile Enyo offered almost singed him with its brightness.

"You're going to do it," he said with disbelief.

"Yup." And with that, she tossed the grappling hook.

He expected it to fall.

But this was Enyo. The assassin. The woman of confidence and brass balls.

The barbs caught the edge of the hole and held. A moment later, she climbed as he held his breath.

Instinct had him suddenly moving only seconds before the grappling hook disappeared, leaving the rope attached to nothing. Enyo plummeted, right into his arms.

"Oof." A sound from both of them that had them staring at each other.

And what did her cheeky assassin ass say? "Nice catch."

Tell that to his still-racing heart.

She wiggled from his grip that she might stoop and grab her fallen rope. The end appeared sheared clean.

"Looks like it was a good thing I didn't have my head in that hole," she quipped.

Knowing said opening disintegrated objects didn't stop her from playing with it. While Dina and Frieda inspected the murals on the wall, Enyo amused herself by tossing things into the hole. Knife went spinning, hilt over blade, entered the hole, and didn't return. A bullet fired into it had no effect.

When she left, he thought her done fucking around, but she returned with fruit. At his raised brow, she explained, "It doesn't like metal or nylon, so I'll try organic matter."

The orange disappeared, as did the coconut.

Once more she disappeared and was gone a little bit longer before returning with a box that chirped.

"Dare I ask?"

She lifted the flap. "Let's see what happens to living things."

The small finches went into a frenzy to escape captivity, flitting around the room, circling higher and higher as they aimed for the spot of sunshine that indicated freedom. The first one went through seemingly without issue. The second hovered midway in the hole. At ten seconds—

Splat.

Half of its body hit the floor.

Enyo pursed her lips. "Well, I guess that answers that question."

He hated to admit her test had been interesting.

Done playing with the hole—which even in his mind sounded dirty—Enyo went to tap on the pillar, first with her fist then the pommel of her knife.

It led to Dina snapping. "Are you trying to break it?"

"If I wanted to try, I'd have brought a sledgehammer."

"Doesn't even chip it," he muttered. Her surprised glance had him wryly adding, "I spent a decade with anger issues and only this room to vent on." He'd taken heavy sledges to the stone column, even gotten a gas-powered jackhammer.

"Magic doesn't work as expected," Dina stated as she neared them. She held out her hand, and it sputtered with sparks. "It's a struggle to maintain any kind of connection to it. Reminds me of being a teenager when I was first learning how to use my power."

"I still feel strong." Enyo flexed.

"But are you as strong?" Dina questioned. "What about your concealment ability?"

A glance around had Enyo stating, "There are no shadows to hide in." A peculiar trait of the room.

Frieda neared them. "Are we done? This place is creepy."

"In a second." Dina held up her hand. "You had a vision in here."

"I have visions everywhere," Frieda retorted.

"I mean, your magic worked. Why not ours?"

"Could it be because she glows yellow?" Enyo pointed to Frieda's back where her tattoos illuminated underneath her shirt.

"Weird, seeing as how we all have the same marks," Dina murmured.

"But different powers." Bane pointed out the obvious.

"Enough work. I am famished. Let's go find some grub." Enyo ended the conversation.

After lunch, Enyo joined Bane as he made his rounds of the island. Talking to folk. Listening to what they'd seen. An afternoon of nothing that had Enyo complaining, "Boring. I can't believe we weren't attacked once."

"Most people would be happy about that."

"I'm not most people, Spot."

Which was proving to be precisely the problem.

21

·)·)·)·⊙·(·(·(·

KEEPING BANE OFF BALANCE AMUSED ME. I hated being predictable, and I could admit a certain glee in seeing how my actions drove him a little nuts.

The incident in the cavern, where the hole ate my grappling hook, had been a sobering reminder that maybe I should tread a little more cautiously than usual. In my defense, I'd never dealt with magic on a job before. Alarm systems, yes. Guards, dogs, even an attack falcon. But having to worry about invisible mojo disintegrating flesh? I might have to change up some of my usual methods.

I spent the dullest afternoon while Bane played king of the island, moving among his subjects. He was well-liked, it seemed, given no one tried to toss any rotten fruit or insults. Not one monster to be seen. I'll admit to being kind of let down.

Supper time proved just as uneventful, if delicious. The chef prepared some kind of saucy meat dish that went over egg noodles with fresh, crusty bread for dipping. Only Frieda choked as she found out we were eating the roc from the attack.

I leaned over and whispered, "Reduce, reuse, recycle."

She ran from the table with a hand over her mouth. I'd done my job as her sister.

After dinner, Bane murmured, "Let's go for a walk on the beach."

The two of us alone, at night, with monsters possibly lurking in wait? Oh, hell yeah.

We headed down from the castle, not saying much, both of us alert. Him especially. His head swiveled left and right. His nose kept flaring.

"Expecting trouble?" I asked softly.

"Aren't you?"

"Always."

"That isn't a way to live," he muttered.

"Says you."

"Yeah, says me."

"Suck it up, Spot. It will be all over in a few days."

"With the countdown to the next starting," was his grim rejoinder.

Our feet kicked up sand as we hit a dry section above the tide line. The ocean had rolled out, leaving a long, wet expanse riddled with seaweed and shells. He paused to stare out over the water, lost in thought.

When he finally did speak, he surprised me. "You and your sisters, this bond you have, what happens if one of you gets married or becomes serious with someone?"

"I imagine they'd have to move into the building so we can stay close."

"Have you ever looked to break the tie?"

"We have. Can't break something no one can see."

"Tell me something I don't know." He shoved his hands into his pockets.

"I guess the same could be said of you. If you meet someone, you'll need them to live on the island."

"I would never do that to someone I cared for."

"What if they wanted to?" I insisted.

He snorted. "Your sister said almost the same thing this morning. The reality is, as you well know, it's not easy asking someone to become part of a curse. To curtail where they can live, what they can do, and, worse, put them in danger."

The conversation held some deeper meaning

that I wanted to explore and didn't at the same time. "They say love conquers all."

"Love also kills," he said abruptly as he turned around. "We should get to bed."

"Aye, aye, Warden."

Our way back remained uneventful. He went to the bathroom, then so did I, laying my booby traps in place. Once more I crawled into bed beside his warm body. Only this time, he'd already turned on his side, giving me his broad back. He didn't sleep, though. Neither did I. I lay, staring at the ceiling, trying to not think of what my sister said. How I'd die because he didn't love me.

As if I wanted love. Who needed that emotion? I knew Bane agreed. He'd seen what love led to with his parents. Grief.

My own mother had eschewed a relationship, choosing to have children on her own terms, never being beholden to anyone. She'd never seemed lonely, and I had to wonder how she did it because some nights when I sat on the couch alone with only my thoughts for company, I wanted to scream, *Is this all there is?* My sisters, and now Bane, questioned why I constantly sought the adrenaline rush, the danger. The answer seemed so obvious: to feel alive.

I rolled out of the bed, leading to him grunting, "What's wrong?"

"Gotta pee."

I trudged for the bathroom, removing the boobytraps from the lid. Nothing in the water. I sat down and let loose, my urine hitting with a splash and a gurgle.

Wait a second. That wasn't right.

I stood not a moment too soon as something exploded from the toilet, aiming for my nether region. As I tried to dodge, the panties around my ankles impeded my movement. I fell with a thump and ass scooched away from the creature hopsliding for me, a cross between a frog and a slug. Want to bet the slime would make me sick if it touched flesh? I eschewed my gun in favor of the plunger, smacking the critter hard enough it flew with a squeal and hit the wall.

Even as it recovered, the toilet bubbled and more came boiling up. I kicked off my panties since I didn't have time to pull them back up and scrambled to my feet. *Whack. Bat. Squeak. Squish.* My violent frenzy left me somewhat spattered with goo as bodies exploded.

I'd no sooner hit the last one than the bathroom door flung open and there was Bane in all his naked glory, ready to do battle.

Me, I was covered in guts.

He eyed me, the mess, and sighed. "And here I thought I was a magnet for trouble."

239

"Oh, Spot. You ain't seen nothing yet."

"What I see is you need a shower before you crawl back into bed."

"A good idea. This stuff is making my skin numb. But first..." I yanked down the toilet seat lid and then used a robe's sash to tie it shut before piling the toiletries on top. "That should make some noise if they try to go through there again."

"Let me ping Lorcan to tell him to do a bathroom check in case other toilets are affected."

"I'll be out in a second. Try to not get killed while I sluice off." He left as I entered the glass-enclosed shower, sending a mental shout to my sisters. *Monsters in the toilet.*

Rather than cast doubt on the strange warning, Dina replied, *Placing a shielding spell on the plumbing for the castle.*

Nice. That would help quite a bit.

To my surprise, Bane returned before I'd managed to rinse off.

I glanced at him through the steamed-up glass. "Everything okay?"

"Lorcan's got his men checking all the drains in the castle. I thought it might be safer if I kept watch while you're vulnerable."

I couldn't help a husky chuckle. "Oh, Spot. Only you would think I'm defenseless while naked."

"Would it kill you to pretend I'm doing something useful?"

"Very well. Please guard me, oh mighty jungle cat, that I might bathe without fear."

Knowing he watched, I might have taken my soaping to a more sensual level than needed. Gliding that bar—which had touched his skin— over my flesh. Over my breasts, with nipples already erect. Between my legs, the friction only serving to tease.

Considering we'd been dancing around our attraction for days, I didn't expect him to react. To my shock—and pleasure—he growled and strode for me, stepping into the shower and dragging me to his chest.

My head was already tilted when his mouth came down on mine for a kiss. More like an explosion to my senses. I lost my breath. My knees went weak. A good thing he held me up.

I wanted to blame the slime, but this was all him. The first and only man to ever make me melt.

He slammed the water off. "Let's go to bed," he rumbled.

Hell yeah. I would have dragged him there, but he had other ideas, sweeping me into his arms and carrying me. Me! As if I were some delicate thing.

He tossed me onto the bed, and while I was mid-bounce, he knelt on the mattress. I landed in a sitting position, eyeing him. Would he change his mind?

He grabbed me by the ankle and dragged me toward him, sensual promise in his gaze. He bent forward and placed his mouth against my inner thigh, and damned if I didn't tremble.

I finally understood the Madonna song. I was like a virgin. Each touch new and exciting. His mouth moved up my leg until he nuzzled my pubes.

And was he— "Are you sniffing me?" I couldn't help but exclaim.

"Fuck yeah, I am. Do you have any idea how delectable you are to me? How I've wanted to taste your sweetness?" He whispered those words against my flesh, and I shivered.

I'd never felt so desired.

So—

My hips bucked as he blew hotly on my sex. Sweet fucking hell. He grabbed hold of me and held me in place as he blew again. It shouldn't have felt so good.

He pushed my legs apart, exposing me to him, making it easy for his mouth to latch onto my needy pussy. Instant zing had me thrusting my hips. But he wasn't a weak man. He flattened his palms against my belly, anchoring me that he might pleasure me.

Oh, how he pleased me. As his tongue delved between my nether lips, I fisted the sheets, trying to not come too fast, but I'd been holding on for days. Days where I'd not had a moment to masturbate for relief. Days of watching him, of wanting him.

He lapped at my sex, paying special attention to my clit, making me pant and moan. I shuddered as he shoved a finger into me as his tongue continued to tease my button.

"Another," I begged.

He slid a second finger in, making it tighter, giving me something to squeeze. I clamped down on his fingers. and he groaned.

"Fuck. Why must you smell and taste so fucking good?"

He kept feasting and teasing, triggering a fast climax that drew an abrupt scream from me. And then he kept playing, drawing out my orgasm, getting my body to tighten even further.

"Fuck me," I begged. "I want to feel you inside me."

My plea worked. His body covered mine, the heat of his flesh on mine making me pant against his seeking mouth that tasted of me. The friction of the hair on his chest on my breasts only made me hotter.

The head of him poked, pushed, thick, hard. I gasped as he penetrated me, stretched me. Filled me. I clawed at his shoulders as my desire overwhelmed.

He pushed deep, seating himself fully, and my whole body quivered, tightened around him, and he uttered a sound.

"This is going to be embarrassingly fast."

"Good." I liked that he was out of control.

My hips rotated, starting a rhythm he soon joined, his short, firm thrusts butting against my inner sweet spot. Pushing. Coiling. The pleasure pressure built, and when I keened in release for a second time, my climax ripping through me, he joined me. Our bodies arched and locked in orgasmic pleasure. Our hearts beating in time. Our minds touching long enough for me to hear his thoughts.

What have I done?

Had I heard him? Or did I imagine his regret? I might have worried about it but for the soft, sensual kiss. A kiss that led to a more leisurely second round, where he explored my body and I learned every inch of his.

We collapsed with limbs entwined afterwards, falling asleep, and this time waking together. Me as the little spoon for the first time in my life. Even more astonishing, I liked it.

22

The Warden

ALL OF BANE'S REASONS FOR STAYING AWAY couldn't keep him from seducing Enyo. He'd heard her under attack and rushed in that bathroom to save her. Only she didn't need his help. She could handle herself.

And that belief would kill her.

Bane thought by remaining aloof he could convince her to leave. When that failed, he'd wanted to keep himself from caring. That also flunked miserably.

With only two days left before the eclipse, he had to wonder why he made them both suffer. Why not indulge in some pleasure before everything went to Hell? He already knew this would end badly. Even if Enyo didn't die, she couldn't live with him on the island, nor could she leave her sisters. Their tenuous relationship had failed before it even began. But he would wring out every ounce of pleasure he could in the meantime.

Rub her. Lick her. But he drew the line at peeing on her leg like his cat wanted. Although if he thought for one second it would protect her from threats, he'd hose her down in an instant.

They woke up entwined, his body pressed against hers, his hard-on poking her backside. When she murmured, "Good morning, Spot," he nibbled her neck as he slid into her, rocking them into a sensual climax.

At breakfast, Dina took one look at them and snorted. "About time."

Time was a thing they had so little of. Preparations had them busy with Enyo barking out orders to the soldiers and anyone else she could bully into obeying. She conscripted soldiers into digging pits on the beach and spiking them. She had barrels of gluey shit prepared and placed at the top of the causeway to the castle. Containers of oil lined the parapets—his idea, actually. He'd seen it in a movie. Pour it over the invaders and light them on fire.

Melisandre recruited some aquatic friends who only wanted to be paid in fish guts and a promise of safety in the island's harbor. Sam... Sam lamented the fact all the prep work would mean less smashing for him.

Bane's friend, Lance, the maker of teleport balls, arrived on the yacht—which Lance declared safe since he'd reinforced the hull. Apparently, someone had used magic to loosen the welds holding it together.

Enyo made it clear she wasn't a fan. As she stated, *"Feels like he's hiding something."*

Her remark had Bane eyeing his friend differently, noticing how often he sneered when he thought no one looked. For a guy who showed up to help, he displayed an awful lot of disdain.

It took one of the sisters to put him in his place. When Lance offered to set up some offensive spells that would trigger if attacked, Dina haughtily replied, "As if I haven't already. Some of us don't show up at the last second and pretend to be useful."

The insult clenched Lance's jaw, and Bane caught the dark look in his eyes. Would he retaliate over a bruised ego? Bane would have to keep an eye on it.

John, however, remained as likeable as ever. Not that Bane had seen him much the last day or so. When not erecting defensive sigils, he had his head buried in books as he sought to find anything that might help.

The only one who kept aloof? Frieda, because as Enyo explained, *"In her mind, this battle is already done."*

A foregone conclusion? He refused to accept it. Just like he refused to see Enyo die. Surely there was something he could do to change Frieda's vision.

They'd not seen a real attack since the roc, unless the toilet frogs counted. The lack of activity by the monsters led to strung-out soldiers and short tempers. Everyone walked on eggshells, tension making them on edge.

And what did Enyo propose that last afternoon?

"Let's fuck."

"Shouldn't we be vigilant?" The weight of responsibility crushed him and soured the words.

"We've done everything we can. So either we goad each other into a fight to burn off some energy or we fuck. What's it going to be, Spot?"

Neither, as he chose to make love to her. Softly. Sensually. He worshipped her body until she cried out his name.

In that moment, as she clung tight to him, he could no longer deny he'd fallen in love.

A love he didn't know how to protect.

Hence why he went to Dina on the morning of the eclipse. She and Frieda stood in the courtyard, chatting softly as he neared.

Without preamble, he stated, "You have to take Enyo away from here."

"She won't leave," Dina stated, casting a glare at a wall and the glyph Lance had placed on it. To Bane it seemed fine, but her expression indicated otherwise.

"I've tried to convince her," Frieda added. "But that might have been the worst thing to do. She can be rather contrary with my advice."

"I don't want her to die," he growled. "There has to be something we can do."

"You love her," Frieda stated, not asked.

"Yes, which is why I won't sacrifice her to my curse. You must help me."

Frieda glanced at Dina, who pursed her lips. "We'll see what we can do."

Relief eased some of his tension. "Thank you."

"Don't thank me yet. Enyo is a stubborn hag. It might require bashing her over the head and carting her off by force."

"At least she'd live."

"We might not, though. You don't want to get on her bad side," Dina warned, to which Frieda nodded.

"You're her sisters. I know you'll do what's right."

Leaving the Grae sisters, Bane went inside the castle and ran into Lance. Bane had made friends with the wizard a few years back during one of his research missions. While Bane had failed to learn anything of import in his digging, Lance had offered to try a few tricks to free him, none of which worked.

Lance had been the first to suggest that maybe he should let the portal open. To which Bane had reacted with horror and his friend replied, *"Chill. Was just a suggestion. It must suck to be stuck here like a prisoner."*

Sure, Lance didn't always say the right thing, but Bane had few friends. Lance had been the one to encourage Bane to find a new bodyguard when his previous ones failed. He had Lance to thank for leading him to Enyo.

Speaking of whom... He'd not seen her since breakfast when she'd left to track down Lorcan to relate some last-minute instructions. She'd not left without a stern warning for Bane, *"Don't you dare leave this castle or go outside."*

"Or else what?" he'd replied.

"Are you asking for a demonstration of my rope skills?"

"You can show me later." Once everything was over and done with. If they both survived.

Fuck, only one hour until the eclipse. One hour until Enyo lived or died. According to her plan, they should be heading into the basement right about now and locking the door shut behind them. Once closed, they'd be safe.

It took him a moment to realize Lance spoke. "...to get ready."

"I'm sorry, what?"

"I said given everyone's in place and prepped for the attack, isn't it time you got ready?"

"What's to get ready? I slap my hands on the portal and keep it closed." Did he detect a tone of bitterness in his words?

"Exactly. You should be down there, not up here, just in case shit hits the fan."

"Not yet. Enyo's not here."

"But she knows where to find you. Don't worry. I can cover your ass while we're waiting for her. We'll leave the gate open. She can shut it once she's inside."

Bane hesitated.

"Might be good to ensure we've got a clear shot to the cavern at the very least."

Lance might have a point, and it wasn't as if pacing the main hall of the castle accomplished anything. "Okay, let's go."

As they headed down, Lance casually remarked, "I'm surprised the assassin stuck around this long. She's known for only taking quick jobs."

That caused him to frown. "Knowing that, why would you have recommended her to me?"

"I didn't actually think she'd pass your tests. Quite a surprise to learn she has arcane sisters and might have a touch of it herself."

Something struck Bane as wrong. He paused by the gate that led to the cavern. "You sent her to me expecting her to fail?"

"At that point, you'd already gone through several prospects. I figured, why not?"

"You had nothing but praise for her and the job she did for your mother." Bane put his hand on the exotic metal, the tingle and warmth familiar as it unlocked.

"I might have oversold her skills. Honestly, anyone could have done it. I offered, but my mother didn't want that mobster's death leading back to me, especially given I already had a few black marks on my record."

A few? Bane hadn't realized there'd been more incidents.

They entered the tunnel beyond, and Bane remained troubled by Lance's assumption Enyo would fail. "Well, it turns out Enyo is more gifted than either of us expected."

"She must be since she managed to get into your pants. You must have been desperate to bang that oversized bitch. Guess you're taking your life in your hands when she gets on top." Lance's laughter had an unpleasant tone to it.

"Don't talk about her like that," Bane growled, clenching his fist. It took everything in him not to tear off Lance's smug face.

"Or what?" Lance taunted.

"What's wrong with you?" he asked. "Why are you being a dick all of a sudden?"

"Why is it being a dick to tell the truth? You were both desperate. It's kind of natural you'd end up fucking."

Bane looked at his friend but didn't see the usually amenable fellow he thought he knew. The sly gleam in his eyes, the sneer...

"I think you need to leave." Bane kept his voice even and low, trying to keep the rage from boiling over.

"What's wrong, Warden? Truth hurt?"

"I've heard enough from you!" Before Bane could take a swing at Lance, cold hit him, a blanketing chill that froze his limbs, his voice.

Fucking magic.

While Bane did an imitation of a dumb statue, Lance grabbed the bars of the gate and slammed it shut, locking it. Then he turned with an ominous smile as he held up a pair of handcuffs. The metal cuffs snapped around Bane's wrists, the silver in them dulling his connection to his raging leopard.

He'd well and truly fucked up. He should have

listened to Enyo when she said Lance was a sneaky bastard.

"Why?" he managed to mutter through mostly frozen lips.

"Because I've spent years waiting for this day. Even longer trying to find out how and why my dad died. Turns out it was here. In the very same event that took your parents."

He blinked as his brain made the connection. "Your dad—"

"Was the one leading the demons during that eclipse. Mom got rid of most of his notes when he was gone, but I did find a few notations saying that whoever released what's inside that portal would gain great power."

"But the world—"

"Can kiss my ass. Now let's go. I want a front-row seat for the show." Lance shoved Bane, and Bane stumbled before catching himself.

He could curse himself for trusting Lance. The only silver lining?

With the door locked, Enyo couldn't join him in death.

23

·))·))·)·⊙·((·((·

I'D BEEN AWAY FROM BANE TOO LONG, YET every time I tried to return to his side, I got delayed by the stupidest shit.

Soldier having a last-minute panic attack. A good slap and a shouted, "Smarten up, pussy," took care of that.

Lorcan and his men got into an argument about whether they should preemptively shift. I pointed out they couldn't fire a gun if the attack came by air. Our compromise: they stripped down to their skivvies.

Then once I'd finally gotten things squared away, my sisters stood clustered by the castle door, lying in obvious wait.

I was already late for Bane. I'd wanted him underground an hour beforehand, and here we were within fifteen minutes of the main event and I didn't even know where the fuck he was.

Judging by the sisters' expressions, apparently, he'd wait a few more minutes. "What's going on? Why do you have a conspiring look on your faces?"

"Us?" Frieda failed at looking and sounding innocent.

"I know what a plotting face looks like." I should know since I saw it in the mirror often enough.

Dina's chin lifted. "Bane requested we get you to leave."

I snorted. "Is he still pulling that shit? I hope you told him to fuck off."

"No. We said we'd try."

"And failed. I'm not leaving." Although I would admit to finding it cute—if annoying—that he cared about my well-being.

"Are you sure this is where you want to die?" Dina asked baldly.

"I'm not dying." I refused to croak. Not when I'd just found something that made me happy. Would that happiness be difficult? Hell yeah, it would. I mean, we were both cursed, but surely we could find a way to make it work. After all, the next hybrid eclipse wasn't for at least ten years. Maybe we could get more of those teleport balls and commute back and forth.

"You really won't leave him, will you?" Frieda commented softly.

"He needs me." And not just because of the portal. He made me happy. Made me feel alive. More than any treasure, I would fight to keep what we'd begun.

Dina sighed. "Well then, I guess that's settled. Kind of had a feeling you were staying, which means we need a plan that doesn't end up with you six feet under."

"And you think less than fifteen minutes to the eclipse is the right time to dump the current one and start from scratch?" I raised a brow.

"We don't have a choice, given we've been betrayed." Frieda dropped that bomb without warning.

"What are you talking about?" I snapped. "And why are you just telling me now?"

"For some reason, I didn't see the perfidy until now," Frieda admitted.

Before I could ask her what she meant, I heard a thump. A glance showed a soldier had fallen from the parapet, and it had to hurt, yet he lay on the ground drooling instead of screaming, which should have been strident, given his obviously broken leg.

"What the fuck?" I muttered a comment that encompassed the fact everywhere I looked, soldiers suddenly fell asleep.

"And so they were slaughtered while they slept..." Frieda's ominous prediction.

"Someone's cast a sleeping spell," Dina grumbled.

"Then uncast it," I exclaimed.

"She says as if it's that simple," Dina muttered as she headed for the closest soldier slumped against a barrel he'd been assigned as part of the sticky-floor defense. I expected her to use magic, but she started with a slap. When that didn't work, she clapped her hands over the sleeping soldier's ears and shouted, "Awake!" to no avail.

I cast an eye at the castle. Bane. Did he sleep as well?

As I went to step inside, Frieda murmured, "The monsters are coming."

My hand went to the sword sheathed down my spine only to change my mind when Dina said, "Overhead!" I pulled a pair of daggers instead as a peek to the sky showed a cloud of flapping bodies moving toward us, almost blotting out the moon that inched toward the sun. Albatross? Roc? Something worse? Didn't matter. Given the imminent eclipse, I had to be somewhere else.

"Dina! We need those soldiers, like now," I barked.

"A second," she huffed. "I'm still trying to figure out how they all got infected."

"The spell was ingested at breakfast," Frieda stated matter-of-factly.

"Doubtful since we all ate it," I noted. The copious amounts of eggs, bacon, pancakes, and more had delighted even as I ate light. Didn't want to be in a food bloat for battle.

"There is one thing we didn't imbibe," Frieda softly noted.

"The energy drink Lorcan gave his men," Dina exclaimed.

Lorcan had betrayed us! I'd kill him myself.

"This will probably hurt," Dina muttered before she started to glow.

The soldier she held jolted alert and screamed, "Ow!"

Expression flat in the face of the scowling soldier, Dina reported, "I know how to wake them."

"Then get to it," I snapped, stalking to the bear of a man lying on the ground within the portcullis. I had my gun aimed at the traitor and was about to fire when Dina yelled, "You idiot, do you really think he poisoned himself before a monster attack?"

My lips pursed. Probably not. But then who?

My gaze roved around, spotting the sleeping bodies: soldiers, townsfolk. I'd just seen John down on the beach with Melisandre, leaving who unaccounted for?

"Where's Lance?" The one person I'd not talked with much. In my defense, I'd been busy fucking Bane.

Frieda's ominous, "On the threshold of death," didn't help.

Enough. "I need to find the Warden. Dina, wake up as many as you can. Frieda—"

"I'm coming with you." A surprise from my usually reluctant sister.

I wanted to tell her no. It was too dangerous, but hadn't I wanted her to be more assertive? To come out of her shell? I gave her a nod. "Let's go. Stay behind me."

Inside, the castle proved eerily quiet. I had no time to search and trusted my instincts to lead the way. I headed for the passage down to the cavern, finding no one along my path, which ended in a closed gate.

A gate only Bane could open. Perhaps he'd not yet gone inside. My gut said otherwise.

"How do we open the door?" I asked aloud, more musingly than expecting an answer.

Only Frieda had one. "Bane's not the only one with magic tying him here."

I glanced at her. "Meaning what?"

My sister's gaze dropped to my waist, more specifically my spine. To the mark. "You're glowing."

A claim that led to me blurting out, "You are too!"

We didn't need to say anything more. In tune with each other, we grabbed hold of the metal, and nothing happened, not until Dina suddenly joined us.

The gate disappeared. Not opened, not broken. Just suddenly gone. I wanted to question, even as I worried. In my plan, we'd closed the gate so the monsters couldn't get in.

"This was always going to happen," Frieda admitted softly.

Sticking around wouldn't fix it, but I did glare at Dina. "You're supposed to be waking soldiers."

"Most are already recovering. Shifters tend to not be susceptible to poisons and spells. Besides, do you really think I'm going to let you face this by yourself?"

I was glad to have her with us. We were always stronger together.

Taking the lead, I raced down the short hall to the next set of stairs.

Tick tock. The eclipse was almost upon us. I

could feel anticipation humming in the air. Danger too.

I burst into the cavern and just about keeled over at what I found. Bane knelt on the floor by the dais, hands handcuffed behind his back. Lance, that treacherous prick, stood in front of the pillar, which glowed softly at our arrival.

I pulled my gun and fired. To no avail. It clicked uselessly. Failed like magic. Dina had her fingers out but could barely manage a spark.

Lance whirled, and his lip curled. "If I'd known what a pain in my ass you'd be, I would have never recommended you for the job."

"Does this mean you're going to one-star me on Yelp?" I sassed as I dropped the gun.

"Laugh all you want. You're too late. The portal's about to open. My dad's life work, about to be achieved." Lance glanced overhead.

I'm sure he meant for my gaze to follow, but I'd seen too many movies to be distracted at a crucial moment. The knife left my hand, and it didn't miss.

Lance staggered and stared incredulously at the blade jutting from his chest. A heart shot.

No goodbye speech. No threats. He dropped dead.

I ran for Bane, who staggered to his feet, blustering, "Fucker spelled me just inside the gate." He gave me his back and waggled his manacled hands. "I don't suppose you have a key."

"No and no time to pick them. Hold out your hands as far as you can from your body." I pulled the sword from the sheath down my spine.

Bane spread the chain taut.

Snick. My blade sliced through the metal links, leaving him with bracelets, but at least he regained his range of motion. I kept my sword out as I barked, "Get your hands on the pillar. We've got your back."

As he headed for the glowing column, Frieda whispered, "They're coming."

Rather than ask who, I pulled a grenade, although I didn't hold much hope given what happened with the gun.

Dina confirmed it. "I doubt your bomb will work. Things work differently in here."

Just in case, I lobbed it when the first of the monsters entered, some kind of cross between a wolf and a pig, shaggy-haired and horned. The grenade hit the ground and rolled, but no kaboom.

Bloody hell. "Get behind me," I cautioned Frieda, who held a blade despite the fear beading her lip and glossing her eyes.

Dina sidled to the side, muttering, "I'm going to see if I can do something with magic just outside the door to slow the tide."

I almost yelled at her to stay. It was one thing for me to die today. I wouldn't allow anyone else to do the same.

I took some deep breaths to steady myself.

I am strong.

I am fast.

I am death.

A mantra I'd learned to center me before a fight. A fight that came roaring for me before Dina could reach the entrance and set a barrier.

I fell into a trance, the one that let me dance and twirl. My entire body moved in rhythm as I ducked, parried, slashed, swiped. I didn't concentrate on one foe, but rather anything in my vicinity.

Hairy arm? Lob it off.

Chest in front of me? Stab it.

Grabbed from the side? Kick.

A pile of bodies, and various parts thereof, littered the floor, and when the wave ended, I took a breath. Even smiled. "That wasn't so bad."

A bloody—but unharmed—Frieda blinked at me. Dina's gaze wasn't on the door but overhead at the hole, which began to darken.

The eclipse had begun.

A glance showed Bane with his hands pressed to the brightly glowing column, strain on his expression probably due to the seam that appeared in the column of stone.

The portal attempted to open.

"Grawr!" My head flicked so fast I whipped myself with the tip of my ponytail. I gaped as demons entered the cavern from the castle above.

One, two, three... Too fucking many. I didn't need to hear Frieda's whispered, "I love you," to know I looked upon the moment of my death. So be it. I'd go out fighting.

With a scream that would have done a Valkyrie proud, I charged.

24

The Warden

THE SHACKLES ON HIS HANDS BOTHERED Bane. The silver in them didn't irritate his skin, not since they'd entered the chamber, but they reminded him of his stupidity and ill-placed trust. Despite Lance's perfidy, at least Bane could do his job. Slap his palms against the pillar while the woman he loved fought at his back.

A part of him didn't want to watch. Watching and not acting went against everything in him. At least he couldn't hear his cat yowling. This was the only place where that other half of him, that constant presence since he was a child, disappeared. He hated it. Hated feeling as if only part of him existed.

"Take that, you smelly pig fucker!" Enyo yelled.

He turned to look over his shoulder and didn't know whether to shake his head in disbelief or cheer. She was absolute beauty in how she moved. The fluidity of her limbs, the way she timed everything.

Duck, jab, pivot, sweep. Every movement perfectly orchestrated. What seemed impossible—too many pig beasts against her one—Enyo accomplished with ease.

Maybe her sister was wrong. Lance lay dead on the floor. Fucking traitor. Bane would have loved to throttle him with his bare hands. The hairy fuckers didn't appear able to get past her guard. They could prevail.

The pillar heated and turned cold at the same time as the room darkened. As per previous occasions, the seam pulsed, an ominous band of black. Pressure from the other side had him pushing back firmly.

He was the key to keep it closed. The bastion against whatever evil attempted to enter from the other side.

Grawr! The monstrous sound, one not heard since the night his parents died, had him almost spinning around.

Demon.

Make that demons. He could only watch over

his shoulder in horror as the big bastards entered, their cloven hoofs striking sparks, their nostrils blasting smoke.

Enyo dragged the tip of her sword on the floor, a screeching sound to draw attention, and when she had them focused on her, she said, "Let's dance, you fuckers."

They rushed her, a much wilier set of foes set on killing the woman he loved even as the portal strained against his flattened palms.

As he held a stupid fucking door, Enyo battled alone. Frieda lay stunned where she'd been knocked by a powerful blow. Dina looked desperate as a pair of demons stalked in her direction.

There were no soldiers.

No rescue.

Enyo did her best as the room turned pitch-black, the pillar the only light. The fist of power that always struck during this time came down and shoved Enyo to her knees. She gasped. A single sound of surprise.

It was his parents all over again. Bane would watch the woman he loved die because of a curse he never asked for. To save a world he didn't actually give a damn about.

Could he live with himself if he didn't act?

No, he couldn't. With a snarl of rage, he

whirled and dove for the dagger that had fallen beside Frieda. The power didn't shove him down.

And it seemed Enyo had been feigning it. As he plunged the knife in the spine of the demon coming up on her left, she stabbed the one on her right. The monsters dropped, and his gaze met Enyo's. Surprise filled her expression.

"The door!" she exclaimed.

"Isn't more important than you."

Her smile was worth the end of the world.

If they lived to see it. The demons weren't done trying to kill them, but at least she was no longer alone.

"Here, have another dagger." She offered him a second blade to use.

A good thing he'd been trained. Having known he couldn't use his leopard in the cavern, Bane had learned to fight, unlike his father.

Back-to-back, they cut a bloody swathe through the demons and went to Dina's rescue. Saving her meant ignoring those rushing past for the pillar.

Flashes of light had him blinking. It took a turn of his head to see what happened. An opening had appeared within the pillar.

The demons ran into the incandescent doorway, throwing themselves through it. To what purpose? He couldn't tell other than he felt something building. A powder keg ripening for explosion.

"We have to get out of here!" Enyo shouted. "Help me grab Frieda."

The monsters ignored them in favor of the doorway, meaning they reached Enyo's sister without harm.

"I've got her." Bane slung the limp Frieda over his shoulder, only to pause by Enyo's side. The entrance to the chamber teemed with monsters. Demons. More of the hairy pig things. Orcs. Goblins. So many of them coming in a rush.

He didn't need Frieda to predict they wouldn't be able to fight their way through.

A glance overhead showed a glowing rim as the eclipse took forever to pass. It should have lasted a minute but it felt like an eternity.

On his shoulder, Frieda stirred and murmured, "Put me down."

He might have argued, but two hands would be better to fight.

Frieda stood facing the portal and not the threat. Before he could wonder at that choice, the pressure in the chamber released. Exploding bolts of lightning emerged from the open doorway, striking everything in the room. Enyo, Frieda, Dina, and himself.

The impact didn't even have him wavering on his feet. The jolt didn't jiggle, but he did smell burning hair. Not his, he should add. The monsters around them dropped, stinking, cooking piles of death.

The triplets, however, glowed.

Enyo laughed. "This is awesome." She held out her hands, flexing fingers that illuminated from within.

The lightning stopped abruptly, along with the light shining from the pillar, a column no longer white. It turned a dull gray. The hole overhead began to show daylight as the moon slipped past.

An ominous creak sounded. A glance showed the column cracking. It wasn't the only thing breaking apart. A chunk of rock fell from the ceiling and smashed, the splinters ricocheting. A sharp piece sliced by his cheek.

"We have to get out before the ceiling comes down," Frieda advised.

Easier said than done. While the monsters in the room had all fried, new ones appeared in the doorway.

Let's play. Bane almost barked in surprise at hearing his leopard. The cavern had lost its power to suppress magic. He shifted, knowing he'd be more deadly as his cat.

A glowing Enyo patted him on the head as she chirped, "There's my big kitty. Highest kill count gets to be on top."

And with that, the assassin he loved went screaming and slashing a path to the exit.

25

·)·))·)·⊙·(·((·(·

WHEN THE DEMONS KEPT COMING, I
expected to die. I'd like to say I'd resigned myself to
that fate but I found myself angry instead. Angry
that our strategy had been undone by betrayal. I
should have seen the perfidy in Lance's eyes. Sensed
it in his soul. Stopped it.

But I hadn't, and all my planning was for
naught. The monsters poured in, and it became a
fight to the death.

Having been part of Bane's dream, I knew what
to expect, that blast of magic that flattened the
room. What I hadn't predicted? That it wouldn't
affect me, so I faked it.

Faked being weak to fool the demons.

Fooled Bane too. He thought I was going to be

killed, but unlike his father so long ago, Bane chose me.

Me, over duty.

Me, over the world. I was totally going to fuck his brains out if we survived, which appeared kind of iffy at the moment. The demons didn't care Bane loved me. But I did.

Together, we fought back-to-back as the eclipse peaked, and my ears threatened to burst.

You know that feeling before a thunderstorm? The air gets staticky and thick. You can feel it tickling your skin, lifting your hair. I'll admit I didn't actually expect to get hit by lightning. And more than once!

Everyone in that room got pierced as the lightning lanced into every living thing. Me. My sisters. Bane. The monsters, who dropped dead, not that I cared because I was kind of busy funneling the energy pouring into me.

It filled me to the brim, and when I thought I might combust, I heard a voice that had no sound, and yet I understood it clearly.

Champion.

With that proclamation, my body jolted. But not painfully. On the contrary, I no longer ached. Strength and fresh adrenaline filled me, along with battle rage.

We would escape this place, and woe to any who got in my way.

When Frieda declared, "We have to get out before the ceiling comes down," I was ready.

I tossed a challenge to my lover, who switched into his cat. A glowing Dina smartly stepped aside as I screamed and ran berserker style at those standing between me and the epic sex I planned to have.

My headlong charge didn't intimidate the monsters, who saw a human wielding a blade and thought there was no threat. They should have run. The magic being gone meant that gun I pulled had no problem firing. Head shot. Head shot.

I dropped demons in my path, not wasting time or bullets. I'd never been more focused and efficient as I kept spinning and shooting.

Turned out, we didn't need to fight the entire way out. Just past the doorway, we ran into a bloody bear accompanied by an equally messy professor.

"The way out should be mostly clear," John declared.

Lorcan led the way, his fat bear butt racing headlong into the stray monsters that dared get in our path. Bane, not to be outdone, leaped past us and joined his furry commander. The pair of powerful beasts tore through the threats, tossing them left and right in a competition of who could be the wildest creature.

It was still me, but I let them have their moment.

The castle around us rumbled ominously. Dina, by my side, muttered, "I can sense a hole where the cavern used to be."

Sense? "Meaning what?" I asked, my rapid jog not leaving me breathless. Not so my sisters, who huffed to keep up.

"Whatever used to be down in that room is no more."

"That kind of announcement really needs ominous music." The last thing I said before we emerged into the main hall and a scene of carnage.

I saw soldiers moving among the bodies, jabbing those that didn't belong, checking to see if any people had survived. I blamed Lance for the needless deaths. The attack should have been repelled at the castle gate.

Too late now. At least we lived.

"Don't stop and stare. Get out!" Frieda yelled. "Now. Run. Run like the devil is on your ass."

I had to admit to being impressed. I didn't think she had it in her. The soldiers fled, and for a moment, Bane paused, big shaggy head glancing at the halls and doorways farther in. I knew what he thought. Did anyone remain?

"Don't you dare die on me now, Spot!" I yelled, grabbing him by the ruff. I didn't have to drag him, but we were the last two to exit the castle.

In the courtyard, parts of the walls showed stress cracks zigzagging. My sisters passed through the portcullis opening, following Lorcan's butt. John hovered at their rear, a man with a long stride who held back as a protector, his hands upraised and glowing as he held a shield over my siblings' heads to prevent any stray detached chunks of castle from hitting them.

As we emerged onto the causeway, the tremors intensified, vibrating the stone under our feet. Despite it being daytime, the two gargoyles woke and took flight away from the destruction. At the far end of the path, those who'd fled before us kept running, some for the village, others for the docks and the boats that might take them to safety.

I just wanted to make it to the end of the bridge before it all came crashing down.

With a groan that no building should ever make, the castle collapsed in on itself. While dumb, I looked over my shoulder and caught it caving in. Saw the wave rippling outward that downed the walls and kept going, crumbling the causeway. We'd never outrun it. I grabbed hold of Bane's body and buried my face in his fur.

Then, because I'd never get the chance again, I whispered, "Love you, Spot."

Dust filled the air as the ground underneath disappeared, and yet I didn't fall. It took me a second to peek around and realize we floated.

We mother fucking floated! All thanks to Dina. My sister looked like a right witch for once, head tilted back, hands slightly out from her sides, glowing like a beacon as she radiated more power than I'd ever seen her use.

She'd saved us all: me, Bane, Frieda, John, and even that fat bastard, Lorcan, who shifted as she floated us to bellow, "Fuck me, I'm a ghost!"

His naked ass hitting the pebbled ground dis-abused him of that idea real quick. He bounced to his feet with a roared, "Fuck me, I'm alive!" and ran off.

The shellshocked group stood clustered and gaped at the hole and rubble where the castle once perched. Not me, though. I still rode the adrenaline high.

It was John who muttered, "I can't believe we survived."

I could. I beamed at Frieda and stuck out my tongue. "Told you I wasn't going to die."

To which she narrowed her gaze and said, "And just for that, I'm not going to tell you what's going to give you food poisoning on your honeymoon."

I gaped. Wait, was she saying...

Bane shifted, so many yummy inches of naked male, and growled, "I can't believe my parents died for nothing. Centuries of Wardens guarding a door that had nothing behind it."

"I wouldn't call that lightning nothing." I flexed, feeling the extra strength coursing in my limbs.

Bane gestured. "Do you see the world ending? My entire life I was told the apocalypse would come if I didn't guard that fucking door."

"Maybe whatever was behind it died?" I shrugged. "It's been centuries after all."

"Whatever. The curse is done. Let's get out of here," he stated.

"Where are we supposed to go?" I asked. "You don't exactly have a hotel in town."

"There are showers and clothing on the yacht."

Wait, an epic fight followed by a cruise? Could this day get any better?

We tromped down the dock to see some vessels gone and others busy being loaded. It seemed the townsfolk finally had enough, a decision aided by the shivering of the island as if it weren't quite done collapsing.

We anchored in sight of the island, close enough to act should something pop up from the collapsed castle. We'd not seen anything emerge from the portal, but with magic, who knew what might happen?

Sam, the ogre stomped up and down the beach but refused to leave as did Melisandre, the mermaid who'd been wounded in battle. But they were the exception. We watched as every single boat that could float took to the waters, crammed with people and stuff, fleeing for the safety of mainland shore. Given some remained still ashore, trotting out furniture and crates, it would most likely take several trips.

As for us, we waited and watched in comfort. The yacht had four cabins, meaning more than enough room for our group. Bane led me to the captain's quarters since John insisted on keeping watch just in case we'd not seen the last of the monsters.

I didn't worry. Frieda had already said we were done fighting for the day. It meant I could concentrate on showing Bane how happy I was he'd chosen me.

The moment the cabin door closed, I stripped. No sooner was I naked than he lifted me, and I wrapped my legs around his waist. He'd not had time to put on any clothes in our haste to leave, which left his cock bobbing just below my sex.

My arms draped around his neck as our mouths met for a torrid kiss. His fingers dug into my ass cheeks as our tongues dueled for supremacy, maybe the only battle I'd ever gladly lose.

He rolled his hips, seesawing his dick along my cleft. Lubing it. Making me hot.

"Stop teasing," I whispered.

His grip tightened as he angled me for penetration. His hard, slick cock parted my nether lips, filling me.

My breath caught at the sheer pleasure of it, how he stretched me. Our kiss became more a meshing of mouths and panting breaths as he thrust. His hardness clenched by my pussy. He grunted as he moved faster and faster.

Oh, faster still, please.

I could feel the pleasure coiling within, sense the tenseness in his frame as he raced for that peak for me. He buried his face in the hollow where my neck and shoulder joined. His lips parted against my flesh.

At the moment of climax, he bit me hard enough to break skin. The intensity thrust me into a screaming climax. My orgasm squeezed, and he followed me into bliss.

An intense moment into which he whispered, "I love you."

I could have been a smartass and replied, "I know." After all, he'd proved it in the cavern. But this was one of those times that deserved raw honesty.

"I love you more."

He barked with laughter, and so did I. We smiled a lot as we showered. Smiled even more when he dropped to give me oral.

When we eventually emerged from our quarters, not only clean but sated for the moment, we found the gang sitting around the table.

All eyes turned to us, and I wondered why until Frieda said, "I didn't hear you having sex."

"I'm sorry. I'll scream louder next time," was my sarcastic retort. Only it hit me a second later what she meant. My eyes widened. "Wait, are you saying..." I shouted a thought at her. *I think you should hook up with John.*

Not a single blush or stammer. I eyed Dina, who shook her head. "Whatever bound us together on a magical level disappeared with the lightning."

For just a second, I felt a pang. What would this mean? How would this affect us? We'd always been together. Then it hit me...

"Wait, does this mean we can travel, like, separately?"

"Guess we'll soon find out, knowing you," was Dina's dry reply.

"Do you think the lighting did it? Kind of wild how it didn't hurt us but fried the monsters."

"It was a burst of magic. What kind, I don't know. What I can tell you is my power is stronger than before." Dina held up her hands, and purple flames outlined them.

"I healed," I stated, holding out an arm that I distinctly remembered had a bite mark.

"And I'm no longer Warden," Bane quietly added.

I wasn't too shocked, given how we'd left the chamber and what he'd said after the collapse. "Are you sure?"

"Yeah. The weight of duty that used to feel so heavy"—he thumped his chest—"is gone."

My smile beamed bright. "Holy shit. Seems like opening the door was a good thing."

"Don't be so sure of that," Frieda murmured.

"Did you see something emerge?" I'd been too busy fighting, but I knew Frieda had been watching.

"No, but it's possible something did. When the lightning hit, I closed my eyes."

"Okay, then let me ask you, do you see the apocalypse happening because we let the portal open?" I poked.

"Nope." Her thin shoulders lifted and fell.

Anyone who didn't know Frieda well would have missed the tiny lie. But we'd shared the same womb. I knew her. Knew she didn't tell the entire truth, but I didn't push it.

When she was ready, she'd tell us. After all, the Grae sisters would always stick together, curse or no curse.

Epilogue

·)·))·)·⊙·(·((·(·

By the following morning, the island had been pretty much evacuated, seeing as how the collapse of the castle was only the beginning of the destruction. As the trembling continued, crumbling the shoreline, and cracking the walls and beams in buildings, the few remaining people who'd remained to pack valuables and personal items crowded the dock. We loaded them and their possessions on the yacht and deposited them at the marina of the nearest town. Our third and last trip included a drunken Lorcan, who'd been dipping his cup in a barrel of beer left behind.

Drunk bear shifter singing off-key? Not a pretty sight or sound, but it wasn't the reason Bane dumped him and the mercs and chose to not stick around. For one, the hotels and every single room for rent were full up. Second, technically Bane wasn't their boss or leader, not anymore at any rate. And third? Bane wanted away. Couldn't really blame the guy. After a life spent in servitude, he was ready to live.

We set sail, putting distance between us and the place that once cursed him, leaving me with one question. Unlike my sister Dina, who kept asking a ton; *Who created the portal in the first place? Why did it have a Warden? Did anything come out of that door?*

My replies? *Don't care. Don't care.* And if something did emerge, I'd kill it because I wouldn't let Bane become cursed again.

"What's the plan, Spot?" I asked as we lounged naked in the captain's bed.

"I don't know."

"How about going somewhere awesome and celebrating the fact you're free?"

"Speaking of freedom, I owe you. Unfortunately, the vault with the treasure I promised is gone, but I do have money in the bank. Tell me how much you want for completing the job."

I snorted. "Nothing. Technically, I didn't keep the monsters away. The portal opened."

"You kept me alive, and a deal is a deal. Not to mention, I am a man who always pays his debts.

What will you take as payment? I don't have any gold or jewels anymore, but I do have money, stocks, and this yacht."

There was only one thing that tempted...

I dragged Bane close and whispered against his lips, "All I want is you."

"I'm already yours." He crushed me to him as he rumbled, "As if I was ever going to let you go. I love you, even if you drive me nuts."

"Ah, Spot. I love you, too." And I'd kill anyone who ever tried to tear us apart.

———

FRIEDA STARED over the water as the yacht chugged along, bypassing the nearby town to head for a larger port. John, the man who confused her, joined her at the rail.

"For someone who survived hell, you look upset."

How to explain the turmoil in her, the way her power had shifted and not for the better? She turned to him and said, "Can I ask you something?" Surely a professor of history could point her in the direction of a book or a scroll of someone with a power like hers. Hell, she'd settle for a stone tablet if she could figure out how not to go insane from the increased influx of visions.

"Anything." His lips curved into a smile that gave her butterflies.

But she had to stay strong and not give in. For one, she was way too messed up for a relationship, and two, she'd seen how them getting involved would turn out. Deadly for him. Heartbreaking for her.

Can Frieda get a handle on her seeing ability and find love?

Guess we'll find out in *Professor and the Seer*.

Made in the USA
Middletown, DE
22 December 2023